"I remember the time your father told me he would skin me alive if he ever caught me with one of his daughters. Scared the living daylights out of me."

A slice of surprise caught at her. "I didn't know he'd warned you off. So that's why you didn't give any of us a second look."

"Oh, I took more than a second look. I just made sure you didn't know it. There were plenty of times I thought about you long after my polite, Jedediah-approved chats with you."

Vivian saw the dark hunger in his eyes she'd been sure she'd imagined all those years ago and her heart started to hammer in her chest while her stomach took a big dip. It was as if she was fifteen again and all she wanted was for Benjamin to look at her. And maybe want her a little so she didn't feel like such a fool.

Benjamin lowered his mouth, inch by excruciating inch. She could hardly breathe and thinking was out of the question. When his lips touched hers, she couldn't stop a soft sigh. He must have taken that as an affirmation because then he slid his hand behind her neck and deepened the pressure, exploring her mouth as if he'd been waiting a long time.

Vivian felt herself sinking into the taste and sensation of his hunger. Her body reacted like lightning, taking her completely off guard.

* * *

HONEYMOON MOUNTAIN: Love on a hilltop!

Dear Reader,

Come with me to Honeymoon Mountain! Picture a mountain lodge overlooking a lake. A dock invites you to stroll to the end of it and maybe even leap into that beautiful water. The view from the screened-in porch changes with the season—lush and green in summer, starkly gray in winter. Memories echo off the hardwood walls and floors of the lodge.

Sounds wonderful, doesn't it? Well, it is except for the fact that it's a big money pit, too.

When the three daughters of Jedediah Jackson—Vivian, Temple and Jillian—reunite after their father's death, they initially decide that the only sensible thing to do is to sell the lodge. But an unexpected event causes an abrupt change in their sensible plans. Still recovering from the humiliating end of her marriage on her honeymoon, Vivian Jackson has buried herself in work. Honeymoon Mountain brings back many memories of visits with her father during the summer, but it also reminds her of her unrequited crush on Benjamin Hunter all those many years ago. Much to her surprise, Benjamin is just as strong and tempting as he was when she was fifteen years old. Now that she is on the receiving end of his undivided attention, Vivian wonders if she should give in to having a fling with Benjamin. The trouble is...will it be a fling or much, much more?

I hope you'll enjoy meeting and getting to know the people in this small town and joining Vivian and Benjamin on their journey, too.

You can contact me at leannebanks.com. I love to hear from readers!

Enjoy!

Leanne Banks

Honeymoon
Mountain Bride

—

Leanne Banks

HARLEQUIN® SPECIAL EDITION®

Recycling programs
for this product may
not exist in your area.

ISBN-13: 978-0-373-62354-9

Honeymoon Mountain Bride

Printed in U.S.A.

Leanne Banks is a *New York Times* and *USA TODAY* bestselling author with over sixty-eight books to her credit. Leanne loves her family, the beach and chocolate. You can reach her at leannebanks.com.

Visit the Author Profile page
at Harlequin.com for more titles.

This book is dedicated to all of you
who encouraged me to write it and finish it!
You know who you are!

Chapter One

"To Dad," Vivian Jackson said, lifting her glass of cheap wine as she looked beyond the dock to the blue waters of the North Carolina lake. "Peaceful sailing."

"Catch the big one," her sister Temple said, lifting her glass.

"To Dad," her youngest sister, Jillian, said. "Drop that eight-point buck with one shot right between the eyes."

Vivian winced at the image but knew her father, Jedediah Jackson, the son of a son of a sailor, retired navy himself and hunter/fisher extraordinaire, would approve.

Although Vivian had never quite thought she'd measured up to her father's expectations, she felt a painful sense of loss. "I almost can't believe he's really gone. I expect him to come down that hill from the lodge with a bait box and two fishing poles, telling me not to be afraid of worms and insects and not to throw the pole in the water when I get a little bite on the line."

"He didn't always know what to do with girls. I think he was hoping for a son," Temple said.

"I'm as close as he got," Jillian said.

Vivian couldn't help but chuckle at her sister's statement. With a bombshell body, bad-girl-red lips, smoky eyes and wild ways with men, platinum blonde Jilly had caused more than her share of their dear dad's indigestion.

"Not close at all," Temple muttered and moved her glass of wine from one hand to the other. She cleared her throat. "I hate to be a mood-killer, but I think we all know what we need to do with the lodge."

Vivian felt a twinge of pain at giving up the lodge, even though it was the practical thing to do. "I didn't think it would bother me," she said, feeling a flood of memories rush through her. Staying with her father in the summers had meant she could get dirty without her mother becoming upset. Vivian had experienced her first crush here at Honeymoon Mountain Lake. The memory was more humiliating than sweet, but she didn't want to give it all away. "Or maybe I just hoped it wouldn't bother me."

Temple gave her a considering glance from behind her glasses. "But you do agree we should sell it.

As it is, it's a money pit. The cabins and main house are in disrepair, and I don't think any of us wants to sink our life's savings into it. Plus, Dad canceled all reservations once he got truly sick. I'm not sure we'll get our regulars back since they had to find another resort for their vacations."

"He was sicker than we realized," Vivian said, feeling regret that she hadn't caught on to his illness. But she was certain Temple, an accountant and financial planner, had done her homework on the best options for their inheritance.

Jilly nodded and tossed back the rest of her wine. "I'm just glad we all got to see him during that last month he was alive. Makes me believe in fate and luck." She sighed. "I have practical skills in many areas, but not enough money to save the lodge."

"Then we're agreed," Temple said. "We're selling it. We may have to accept a low offer due to the condition of the property."

"I didn't ever expect to get any money out of it, anyway," Jilly said.

Vivian put her arm around her youngest sister. Jilly talked and acted tough, but she had a tender heart about some things.

"I'll find a real estate agent, but someone needs to tell the full-time employees." Temple looked expectantly at Vivian.

Vivian frowned. "Why me?"

"You're the oldest," Temple said.

"What does that have to do with anything? In fact, I think you would be the perfect one to deliver the news since you're so eager to get rid of the lodge."

"I don't like it any more than you two do, but someone has to be practical, and as usual, that someone is me," Temple said. "I don't want to overthink or overfeel this."

Vivian understood what Temple was saying. Even though Temple could seem cold and calculating, underneath it all, she was suffering, too.

Vivian took a deep breath. "Okay, I'll do it," she said. "But it's not going to be fun. Do you think we'll be able to find a home for Jet?" she asked, thinking of her father's hound dog.

"It's gonna be tough. Maybe Grayson will take him." Grayson was the lodge's handyman and bartender. Temple extended her glass toward Vivian. "You want my wine?"

Vivian rolled her eyes. "This is going to be hard." She hated to think about how the permanent workers would receive the news. After all, they'd been more like family than employees.

"Wish me luck," Vivian said, snatching Temple's glass and downing the contents.

"Luck," Temple and Jilly said together, but Vivian felt not a lick of comfort.

Vivian winced at the bittersweet taste of the cheap wine. As much as she wished differently, the alcohol content wouldn't build her fortitude. She would have to find it in herself.

"Here we go," Vivian muttered and trudged up the hill to the lodge. Grayson and Millicent, the housekeeper, had worked at the lodge before her father had taken it over when his father passed away. It didn't seem fair that the two of them should be booted off the property at this point, but Vivian felt it was only right to give them as much warning as possible. She and her sisters could request that Millicent and Grayson remain employed by the new owner for a limited time, but any reprieve would be temporary.

Climbing the steps to the large dock furnished with all-weather chairs and three well-worn tables with umbrellas, she paused and took a deep breath. She could do this, she told herself. She *would* do this.

Vivian's discussion with Millicent and Grayson hadn't gone well. Both had started to cry. Grayson revealed both he and Millie had spent their retirement savings at a casino. Millie grew so restless Vivian feared the woman was going to break down.

Distraught, Millie requested that Vivian drive her into town to provide a diversion. An hour and a half later, Vivian had carted Millie to the new big-box store, a wine shop and a convenience store to buy lottery tickets. "I need as much luck as ever after today," Millie said as she got back in the car. "I just want to make one more stop. A couple of beers with my friends should cheer me up. Honeymoon Bar."

Vivian twitched at Millie's final request. Years and years had passed, but when they were teens, Vivian had once suffered a major crush on the man who now owned the Honeymoon Bar. She remembered the summer she'd done her best to get Benjamin Hunter's attention. All to no avail. She felt the heat of embarrassment as she remembered his rejection.

"You sure you don't want to go back to the lodge?" Vivian asked. "You have wine."

"That won't help me like a visit with friends," Millie said. "I won't be long. Just a beer or two."

Vivian stopped to let Millie out at the front door, then parked along the street. Perhaps she could just sit in the car and kill some time checking her email. Pulling out her cell phone, she answered messages and deleted all the useless, impersonal advertisements. She glanced at the outside of the bar again and drummed her fingertips on her steering wheel.

So, what was she going to do? Hide in her car for an hour because she was afraid of coming face-to-face with Benjamin Hunter? That was ridiculous. She was a grown woman. She'd dated several men since then, even gotten married, although that had been a disaster from which she was still recovering.

Shaking her head at herself, she pulled together a molecule of the gumption she'd inherited from her father, strode into the bar and looked around. Millicent, along with a small group of people, sat at a table. A few men sat at the bar while they sipped their beers and watched the game on the wide-screen television. An older man tended the bar.

No sign of Benjamin. Her twinge of disappointment irritated her. Stepping deeper into the large room decorated with sports photos and memorabilia, she noticed a sign—Outdoor Seating. The idea appealed to her. After the events of the day, she felt as if the walls were starting to close in on her. She wandered outside and approved of the wrought iron tables and still-green plants and small trees, a courtyard at odds with the good ol' boy bar.

Sinking into one of the chairs at a table, she let out the pent-up breath she'd been holding for way too long. She drew in the scent of a moonflower blooming as the sun began to set and closed her eyes to savor the peaceful moment.

"Would you care for something to drink or eat?" a voice asked, drawing out of her reverie.

Vivian blinked and nodded at the female server. "White wine," she said, assuming the choices were minimal. "Whatever you have."

The server proceeded to name an impressive list. "Pinot Grigio and water," Vivian said. "Thank you."

"I'll be right back," the server said, then walked into the bar.

Vivian raised her eyebrows. Benjamin had definitely made the bar more classy. The last time she'd sneaked in here, she remembered the place as rough and rowdy. Not so tonight. Then again, it was Thursday night. Maybe the weekends were different.

No matter, she thought. Maybe she should take the moment to take a breath. Leaning back in her chair, she closed her eyes again and heard the distant sound of the ball game on TV, but also the sound of a soft breeze rippling the leaves. She concentrated on that, enjoying the peacefulness. But then her restlessness grabbed at her again and she stood, wandering around the small courtyard.

"Pinot Grigio," a deep male voice said, and she instantly knew it was Benjamin.

Vivian turned around and stared into the brown eyes of Benjamin Hunter. She took in the whole of him in one glance. Unfortunately, he had not become soft and potbellied. In fact, he was leaner and harder than she remembered, and somehow his shoulders seemed even broader.

"Hi, Vivian," he said, giving her glass to her as he studied her face. "I'm sorry about Jedediah."

She swallowed and tried to find her voice. Why did she suddenly feel fifteen again? "Thanks. I got to see him a week before he passed. None of us really realized how sick he was even though he made sure we all came to see him," she said and took a sip of her wine.

"He told me," Benjamin said.

A slice of resentment cut through her. "He did?"

"Just a few days before he passed. He made me swear not to tell anyone."

She took a deep breath and nodded. "That sounds like him. I'm just glad my sisters and I got to see him one last time. We're here this weekend, too. Since he didn't want any kind of memorial service, we toasted his memory on the dock."

"That's what he would have wanted," Benjamin said.

"I know," she said. "It just feels odd not to have an official service."

"I think he liked the idea of drifting away. People are going to miss him. He taught me a lot about fishing and some about being a man. Since my father wasn't around much, that counted for a lot. Lord knows I could have gotten into a lot more trouble than I did." Benjamin chuckled to himself. "I remember the time he told me he would skin me alive if he ever caught me with one of his daughters. Scared the living daylights out of me."

Surprise caught her off guard. "I didn't know he'd warned you off. So that's why you didn't give any of us a second look."

"Oh, I took more than a second look. I just made sure you didn't know it. There were plenty of times I thought about you long after my polite Jedediah-approved chats with you."

Vivian saw the dark hunger in his eyes she'd been sure she'd imagined all those years ago, and her heart started to hammer in her chest while her stomach took a big dip. It was as if she was fifteen again and all she wanted was for Benjamin to look at her. And maybe want her a little so she didn't feel like such a fool.

"I always regretted not…" His voice trailed off. "No one here to throw me in the lake. I'd say we're overdue. What's one kiss?"

Vivian stared at him in shock. He wasn't really going to—

Benjamin lowered his mouth, inch by excruciating inch. She could hardly breathe, and thinking was out of the question. When his lips touched hers, she couldn't stop a soft sigh. He must have taken that as an affirmation, because then he slid his hand behind her neck, deepened the pressure and explored her mouth as if he'd been waiting a long time.

Vivian felt herself sinking into the taste and sensation of his hunger. Her body reacted like lightning, taking her completely off guard.

"Mr. Hunter," a male voice called from behind Benjamin, throwing cold reality at her.

Vivian stumbled, backing away and staring at Benjamin. She didn't know if she was more surprised by his action or her reaction to him.

Not turning from her, Benjamin responded. "Yeah, what do you need?"

"You got a phone call. Somebody wants to hold a party here," the server said.

Benjamin glanced over his shoulder. "Thanks. Take a message. Get the number. Tell them I'll call right back."

He turned back to Vivian, and she was thankful the darkness would cover the heat in her cheeks. "I—uh, I need to go. I just brought Millicent into town because her car isn't working properly." She tugged at her purse. "I'll just pay for my wine."

"It's on me," he said.

She took another deep breath, still trying to get rid of her jitteriness. "Thank you. I'll be going, then."

"I look forward to seeing you around town," he said.

She shook her head. "No. My sisters and I have decided to sell the lodge."

He lifted his eyebrows. "Sorry to hear that."

"Yeah, no," she said, discombobulated. She needed to get away.

Chapter Two

"I'm glad I stopped in to see my friends at the bar. Cheered me up. I coulda used just one more beer," Millicent said, her words slightly slurred.

Vivian thought Millicent appeared to be quite relaxed, so she tried to make easy conversation. "I haven't visited the bar in years. It looks like Benjamin has made several changes."

"Oh, yeah," Millicent said and hiccupped. "He's a go-getter. He would have made it far if his mother hadn't taken ill when he was in college. And then his sister…"

Benjamin's family was none of Vivian's business. "His sister?" she prodded, because she couldn't resist.

"Well," Millicent said, "she's gotten into trouble a few times."

"Hmm," Vivian said, remembering that Benjamin hadn't talked about his sister much when they were younger. "I saw him briefly at the bar."

"He's nice enough, but he gets one lady friend, then moves on to the next. I heard he was engaged a long time ago and got burned. Never recovered from it. He's handsome, but he's not the kind to rely on. Your father would tell you the same thing," she warned her.

Vivian, however, was filled with more questions and curiosity than ever. What did Benjamin's sister do to get into trouble? What had happened during his engagement? Who were all these lady friends?

And why did she care?

Vivian tamped down her curiosity and drove up the mountain to the lodge. She had enough on her mind. She didn't need to add Benjamin to the mix.

Benjamin returned to the bar, wondering what in hell had possessed him to kiss Vivian like that. She was still beautiful in a classy, natural way. Honey-blond hair, blue eyes, creamy skin that burned far too easily and a full pink mouth that had always tempted him. He shook his head. Must have been all those years of denial and restraint, he told himself, and picked up his messages as he headed for his office.

One message was from the McAllisters. They wanted to hold a party on a Sunday night. That would work, he thought. He just couldn't set aside Fridays or Saturdays unless it was a dead weekend.

The second message was from his sister. His heart clenched. "Please come get me," the voice mail from Eliza said. "I ran out of gas."

Benjamin took a deep breath. She seemed coherent. He could only hope she was okay.

Benjamin immediately responded to his sister's message. His stomach clenched as it always did. "Eliza," he said. "Are you okay?"

"I'm mostly good," she said. "But I decided to go for a ride and ran out of gas."

He stifled a groan. "Where are you?"

"I think I'm about twelve miles south of town," she said. "I'm on Route 33."

"Okay, I'll head out. How much charge do you have on your phone battery?"

"Not that much," she said. "Sorry. I just needed to take a drive. I was feeling cramped."

Benjamin nodded. He had heard this story before. "I'm coming for you. Don't use your phone for anything else."

He walked to his SUV and started toward Route 33. He hoped Eliza was okay, but she didn't seem overly panicked. She struggled with her illness, but she had seemed fairly even lately. Driving freed his mind from busy work enough to also think about his unexpected meeting with Vivian. Although he'd been tempted, he'd never thought he would kiss her. If he had, he'd never thought it would affect him after all this time. But it had. It damn well had.

He continued driving south on 33, but his mind

kept gravitating back to Vivian. Why had her lips felt so good beneath his? Why did he want to kiss her again? No single encounter with a woman had affected him like this in a long time.

He shook off his thoughts. He would wake up tomorrow and put the whole thing aside. Right now, he needed to make sure his sister was okay.

Benjamin saw the headlights of his sister's vehicle on the side of the road and pulled over. He got out of his SUV with the gas can he kept in the back of his car and strode toward her, immediately filling her tank. "Are you sure you're okay?" he asked.

His younger sister was wide-eyed and restless, but she nodded. "I'm okay."

"You don't look it," he said.

She twisted her mouth. "I'm working on it."

"Next time, call me before you leave the house," he said, escorting her to her car.

"You ever just want to get in your car and drive forever?" she asked.

"Yeah, but there are people counting on me," he said.

"You've always been the responsible one," she said as she climbed into the driver's seat.

"You're getting there," Benjamin said. "You told me you're becoming. You're on a journey."

"Getting there?" she echoed with a laugh. "Sometimes I'm not sure about that."

"Becoming," he said. "You're becoming. We're all damn becoming."

She met his gaze and grinned. "You believe in me when you shouldn't."

"I believe in who you are becoming," he said. Someone had to believe in her so she could believe in herself.

"I'll keep working on it," she said. "Thanks for coming for me."

Benjamin took a deep breath, got in his car and followed his sister home. On the way, however, his lips burned as he remembered kissing Vivian. She tempted him now more than ever. More than that time she'd invited him into the lake to skinny-dip with her.

He gritted his teeth and shook his head. Vivian was not in his future. She wasn't for him. She never had been, and she never would be. He had responsibilities, and he'd learned the hard way when his fiancé had ditched him. His obligations and life in this small town would cramp the style of a Southern flower like Vivian.

After Vivian arrived at the lodge, she went to her room and took a shower. In other circumstances, this might have been an opportunity to reconnect with her sisters, but between her outing with Millicent and her encounter with Benjamin, she felt tapped out. All she wanted was a good night's rest. It took mere seconds for her to fall asleep.

A few hours later, a sharp rap on the door abruptly awakened her. Vivian jerked upright in her bed.

"Missy! There's been a fire," Grayson called from the other side of the door.

Panic raced through her. "Oh, no. Please come in. What's wrong?"

The door opened and Grayson lifted his hands in distress. "There's a fire. One of the cabins is burning."

"No! No!" Alarm hit her like icy water. "Did you dial emergency?"

"The fire department is on the way, but I don't know if they'll get here in time."

"Let me get dressed and I'll come right out." Grayson left the room and she traded her pajamas for a pair of jeans, T-shirt and jacket.

Vivian raced down the hall past Grayson and pounded on Temple's room. Within a few seconds, Temple jerked open her door. "What's going on?"

"A fire in one of the cabins," Vivian said. "Get Jillian."

Vivian raced out the back door of the lodge, down the steps and across the back lawn to the cabin that was burning. She stared at it, wishing she could douse the fire. Thank goodness there were no guests. Surely she could do something.

Before she knew it, she felt Temple grab one of her hands. Jillian took her other hand. She stared at the fire and knew her sisters were staring into it, too.

"Why is it taking so long for the fire department to get here?" Jillian asked.

"We're too far away," Vivian said. "Up the mountain, and they're down in the valley."

"They should be able to get here faster," Jilly said helplessly.

She and her sisters clung to each other as they watched the cabin burn. A fire engine finally arrived and sprayed the cabin, but it was too late. The cabin was a smoldering ruin.

Vivian couldn't explain it, but her heart was broken. Grayson came to her and shook his head. "I'm so sorry. I tried to keep everything in the lodge up to code, but the last couple of years, Jedediah didn't want to overspend on the cabins, and he just didn't seem to have the energy."

Vivian took a deep breath. She knew the wiring for the cabins was primitive at best. She put her hand on his. "I'm just glad no one was in there tonight."

Grayson nodded. A fireman approached her and Grayson, asked a few questions, filled out a report and left.

Exhausted, Vivian returned to the lodge with her sisters.

"Let's have something to eat," Jillian said and urged the three of them to the kitchen.

"I'm not that hungry," Vivian said.

"Neither am I," Temple added.

"You will be in a few minutes," Jillian said and placed a pan on the stove top. Soon she was frying potatoes, bacon and eggs. She placed plates in front of Vivian and Temple, then served herself.

Vivian tried but couldn't take a bite. She closed

her eyes and opened them. "I'm not sure I want to sell," she whispered.

"I don't want to, either," Jilly said and shoveled a forkful of food into her mouth.

Temple gaped at both of them. "Are you out of your minds? This place is a money pit."

"Maybe. Probably," Vivian said. "But I can't let it go yet. Especially after tonight. The whole place feels like an elderly relative and I can't stand to see the whole place go down. We couldn't save Dad. Maybe we can save the lodge."

"Even though we may need to fix the wiring in the cabins?" Temple asked.

Vivian's stomach twisted because she knew Temple was the most financially astute of the three of them. "Yep," she said.

Temple groaned. "Everything about this is wrong. I've studied this six ways from Sunday, and we're going to have a very tough trip to make it successful."

"So, you're saying we *can* make it successful," Jilly said.

Temple frowned at her. "It's an outside chance."

"I think it's a chance I have to take," Vivian said.

"Me, too," Jilly said and shoveled another big bite into her mouth.

Temple sighed, looking from one of them to the other. "Well. Against my better judgment."

"You're in," Jilly said, clapping her hands.

"Let her finish," Vivian said. "I want to hear her say it."

Temple sighed. "I'm in."

"Yay," Jilly said, and gave a hoot of victory.

"That said, I'll be watching every nickel and dime," Temple warned. "Every nickel and dime."

"I guess that means I can't write off pedicures," Jilly said.

Vivian snickered, but Temple squeezed her forehead as if she were in pain.

After an extensive discussion with a local electrician, it appeared that all the cabins might require rewiring and possible plumbing repairs. The job of fixing one cabin was growing by the minute. Vivian went into town, concerned because the man she'd called wouldn't commit to putting a priority on the full project if necessary. Plus there was the issue of choosing new fixtures to replace the out-of-date ones.

She walked into the Honeymoon Hardware store and headed toward the electrical section. Staring at the array of fixtures, she felt overwhelmed. There were even more choices here than online.

"Hey, how ya doing?" asked a male voice from behind her.

Vivian's stomach clenched. She knew that voice. She knew it was Benjamin's. She took a deep breath before she turned to face him. "Hello. What are you doing here?" she asked.

"I could ask the same," he said. "I'm picking up some paint for the kitchen at the bar. What about you?"

"I can't decide on anything. And I need a faster electrician."

"I can help with that," Benjamin said. "I've got the fastest electrician in town."

"How did you find him?" she asked. "Everyone wants to charge us extra because we live on the mountain."

"Give the guy a room while he does the work," Benjamin said. "He can enjoy the amenities when he's off the clock."

Vivian blinked. "Why didn't I think of that?"

"Because you don't fish or hunt," he said.

Her stomach took a dip as she looked at him, but she sure didn't want that response. "I guess you're right. But I still need to choose the fixtures."

"Choose the most long-lasting, not the prettiest," he told her. "Just a thought," he added.

Vivian nodded. Sounded like words of wisdom to her. She made notes as she walked down the aisle.

"I heard about the fire. Sorry."

"Thank you. It was upsetting to say the least."

"Tough timing," he said.

She nodded. "So," she said, feeling a bit awkward, "I didn't get to ask you about how you've been. The bar seems to be doing well. What about you?"

"I'm good," he said. "I've purchased a couple of businesses other than the bar, so that keeps me busy."

"What about your sister?" she asked, remembering what Millie had told her.

Benjamin seemed to freeze.

Vivian took a big step backward internally and gave a shrug. "I have two sisters and you have a sister, and I thought it was just considerate to ask about yours. I never met her because I was always at the lake."

His shoulders lowered just a bit. "She's doing okay."

"Millicent told me your sister is creative and artistic. Maybe she could create something for the lodge."

Benjamin tilted his head from one side to the other. "Maybe. So, your sisters are all in about you fixing the lodge? The last time I talked to you, you said you were leaving."

"Jilly and I are in. We are dragging Temple. She's an accountant, but after the fire, it just didn't seem right to abandon the lodge."

"I'm impressed that you're going to try to fix it. Your dad would be proud," he said, his gaze locking with hers.

"I'm scared. Especially financially."

"You can make it happen. I'll help you when I can," he said.

She felt a sense of relief. "I'll accept that offer, and since you're here, help me select fixtures. Yes?"

"Sure, if you'll go for coffee with me afterward," he said.

Her stomach dipped at the intent expression on his face. It was just coffee, she chided herself and shrugged. "Why not?"

Chapter Three

"So, how do you feel about living in such a small town?" Benjamin asked after they sat at a small table in the local coffee shop.

"I'm okay with it for now," Vivian said. "I'm still telecommuting with my firm in Atlanta and will have to return for some major events. Eventually I'll need to cut the ties. I'm actually kinda glad to get away from the big city."

"Really?" he asked and took a long draw from his cup. "You didn't like Atlanta?"

"I did and didn't," she said. "Who would love that traffic? At the same time, I loved the sense of history and culture. I was raised in Richmond, so of course I loved that city."

"Why not go back to Richmond?" he asked.

She shook her head. "Oh, no. No. My mother lives there and that would be an invitation to…well…insanity, in the worst way."

"That bad?" he asked.

She nodded. "Yes. Well, she's quite the perfectionist." She took a breath. "But enough about me. I still can't figure out why you didn't go pro with football."

"My mom was sick."

"I heard about that. I'm sorry. But after that," she said. "Couldn't you have gone pro after that?"

"I had other obligations by then," he said, his expression moody.

"Do you wish you had continued playing?"

He shrugged. "Depends on the day. Mostly not. It would have been physical torture. Why all the questions?"

She laughed. "My first opportunity. I barely got to talk with you when we were teens."

He chuckled and seems to relax just a smidge. "Yeah, that's true. Speaking of getting to know you, I'm glad you're fixing the lodge, but I'm wondering if you decided to take on fixing Honeymoon Lodge out of obligation," he said.

She thought about that for a moment, then shook her head. "No. Not for the most part. I think we're not ready to let go of our memories and what we experienced here. It took the fire to bring back how important those memories are to us. At the same time, we want to make it better for those who are new visitors to the lodge. It's tricky."

"Yeah, I guess so. If you want it to be more than a fishing and hunting lodge," he said.

"We do," she said. "We think you can still enjoy the lake and the scenery even if you don't hunt or fish."

"Because you don't like worms," he added with a mischievous glint in his eyes.

"Or crawdads," she said. "The lake and the mountains are still beautiful. A walk along the lake will rejuvenate you," she said.

"Even if you hate worms," he said.

She glowered at him. "Yes. Even if you hate worms. Or cocky men who need to be taken down a notch."

"You couldn't be speaking of me," he said.

"Of course not," she lied.

He laughed loudly, and she really liked him for it.

"Viv, you have a lot more kick than I thought you would," he said.

She rolled her eyes. "Benjamin, how could you expect anything less from Jedediah Jackson's daughter? My middle name is Monterey after the aircraft carrier. Eleven battle stars. My father was determined we wouldn't be wussy women, and he was big on Navy history. Each of our middle names is from an aircraft carrier. As for me, I've tripped and fallen a few times, but I've gotten back up."

Benjamin's eyes widened. "Monterey," he echoed. "I'm impressed. Does that mean I can call you Monty?"

"Only if you want me to clock you," she said.

"I'm bigger than you are," he said.

"I'll catch you when you're sleeping," she returned.

"I can only hope," he said. "If you catch me when I'm sleeping, that means you'll be sleeping with me."

A shiver rushed through her, all the way through her core. "Well, that's not going to happen," she said, because it couldn't and shouldn't. She might have been playing with the idea of flirting with Benjamin, but something inside her told her Benjamin was trouble for her. He appeared to be a pillar of the community and an all-around great guy, but for her, he could be big, big trouble. He could be a distraction to her and she wasn't ready for that kind of distraction, especially now that she needed to focus on the lodge.

Benjamin walked her to her car. She took a deep breath and searched for her sanity. "Thanks for your help with the fixtures. And especially your recommendation for an electrician who can do speedy work," she said.

"Glad I could help," he said, leaning toward her.

She instinctively held her breath. "Thanks again," she managed.

"Let's get together again. Saturday," he said. It wasn't a question.

Vivian bit her lip and shook her head. "I don't think that will work," she said.

"Monday?" he asked.

Her lungs seemed to compress, and she shook her head again. "I'm not sure this is a good idea," she managed.

"What's not a good idea?" he asked.

"You and me," she said.

"Maybe we could finally get to know each other," he said, lowering his head.

He took her mouth in a kiss.

Vivian pulled back. "You have got to stop this," she whispered and walked away, her body in complete chaos.

Vivian huddled with Temple and Jillian on the screened-in porch. Temple was glued her laptop and Jillian was trying a new yoga pose. "I ordered fixtures with the help of Benjamin," Vivian announced.

"How did that happen?" Temple asked, clearly suspicious. "Did you arrange to meet him?"

"I did not," Vivian said and wished her cheeks wouldn't heat. "He was at the hardware store and I took advantage of his expertise. Should I not have asked for his advice?"

Temple met her gaze. "Of course not. But I must ask, is he as hunky as ever?"

"I'd like to say he isn't, but I would be lying," Vivian said. "It doesn't matter, though, because we have too much to do for me to be distracted by an ex-football star."

"He's more than an ex-football star, isn't he?" Jillian asked. "He's the town entrepreneur."

Vivian frowned. "He is, but we can't be distracted. Right?"

"Right," Temple said.

"So, we have fixtures ordered. I scheduled a consultation with a plumber. And in other good news, we'll offer a room to an electrician. While they are performing repairs, they can go fishing or hunting in their off hours."

Temple mused. "That could work."

"I wish I could claim it as my idea, but Benjamin suggested it," she said.

"Well, perhaps we should consult him more often," Jillian said.

"I think this is enough for a start," Vivian said, because she didn't want Benjamin around to distract her. She and her sisters needed to get the lodge up to code as soon as possible. "In the meantime, I'd like us to work on the decor for the cabins."

"Decor?" Temple echoed. "We don't have money for decor," she said firmly. "I'm looking at our budget, and we're squeezed tight as it is."

"This may require an investment from all of us. I'm willing to contribute," Vivian said.

Temple tightened her lips. "I don't want to go overbudget."

"What budget?" Vivian asked. "We don't even have one yet."

"Well, we need one," Temple said. "And we should stick to it. This could get totally out of hand."

"Let's just look at the cottages and brainstorm," Vivian said, opening the door from the screened-in porch.

"I don't like this," Temple said, but the three of them walked down to the cabins.

Vivian stepped inside the dark, musty interior of

the first. "They need wallpaper, a complete freshening, mold abatement, modern air-conditioning, new minikitchens and beds. Definitely new beds."

"No to the wallpaper," Temple said. "It's just an invitation to more refurbishment."

"I can paint," Jilly said enthusiastically, lifting her hand. "I've even been paid for it."

Vivian looked at her youngest sister and wondered what in the world she'd done for the last five years that included being paid for painting. She nodded and placed that fact in a file to think about at 2:00 a.m. when she awakened as she so often did. Unfortunately insomnia had recently become Vivian's friend. "Thank you. That's wonderful. But the AC, minikitchens and—"

"Whoa, whoa, whoa," Temple said, lifting her hand. "These aren't luxury villas. They're cabins. Rustic cabins."

"Do you want to stay anywhere that doesn't have heat and air-conditioning, the ability to cook some food and a good mattress for sleeping?"

Temple frowned, then sighed. "We can work on the heat and AC. No to the full kitchens. I'll price stove tops and microwaves."

"And mattresses," Vivian said.

"I suppose," Temple said, clearly unhappy.

"Don't forget the paint," Jilly said. "We don't have to make these luxurious. A lot of people are trying to get back to nature.

"Just so you know I may not want to camp, but I can do it," Jillian said and walked out the cabin door.

"That girl worries me. I wonder if she's been in some kind of trouble that we don't know about," Temple said, staring after her.

"Me, too. I'm afraid of what she's been doing the last few years. I should have kept in touch better."

"I should have, too," Temple said. "I think Mom did a real number on her. I mean, more of a number than she did on you and me."

"We should take her into town for lunch," Vivian said. "Lunch with no distractions about the lodge. We could ask her more about what's been going on in her life."

Temple shot her a dark look. "You think *lunch* will fix anything? That almost sounds like Mom."

"That was insulting and unnecessary," Vivian said. "I think you know I'm different than Mom. Although I wouldn't mind having her best strengths without her weaknesses," she said, thinking of how socially adept her mother was.

"You're right," Temple said. "Lunch it is. We can make it a goal after we've painted one of the cabins."

"That's perfect," she said. "Thank you."

Temple met her gaze. "The numbers don't add up for this," she said. "I keep trying, but—"

"I'll add my savings," Vivian said.

"But what about your retirement?" Temple asked.

"I guess I'll just work till I die," she said with a laugh.

"That's how you're different than Mom," Temple said. "She would rather marry money than work for it."

"It might look like she's had a free ride, but I don't think she has always been happy. She's been paying for that second marriage ever since she took her vows with the good doctor."

"I never thought of it that way, but now that you say it… Hmm," Temple said.

"She wanted her girls to be taken care of," Vivian said.

"But Dad wasn't broke," Temple said. "He could have afforded our college education."

"Mostly," Vivian said. "You and I got scholarships."

"Jilly was always a wandering soul." Temple paused. "Oh, Lord, I hope I never feel like I have to marry for money."

Vivian looked at her slim sister with shoulder-length brown hair. She wore baggy jeans, a T-shirt and black-framed glasses she was always pushing up her nose. Temple was too intelligent to suffer fools gladly. Her hair hung in dark strands down to her shoulders.

"I don't think that's in your near future," she said.

Temple seemed to snap out of her reverie. "Are you saying I'm no bombshell?"

Vivian lifted her hand. "You are formidable and beautiful. Most men couldn't begin to handle you."

"Another way of saying I'm not suitable for anyone," Temple said and started toward the door.

Vivian touched her sister's shoulder. "Another way of saying you deserve someone amazing."

Temple's expression softened. "How'd you turn

out so nice when Mom was so sharp she cut you nearly every day when we were teenagers?"

Vivian smiled, but she knew her expression was stiff. "I took the first cuts," she said.

"Why don't you hate her?" Temple asked.

"A little therapy didn't hurt. I think she did her best. Her best wasn't yours or mine or Jilly's."

Temple sighed and left the cabin.

Vivian felt her tight shoulders slump. This was becoming about so much more than saving her father's lodge. Far more than she knew or was ready to face at the moment. All she knew was that she was all in. Vivian wanted her sisters back, and she was growing surer by the day that this was the way she could get them.

Five days later, Benjamin's recommended electrician had arrived and appeared to be fishing far more than he was wiring. Vivian thought about calling Benjamin, but instead conjured her father's spirit and rose early to confront the electrician, Bill, as he was headed out for another fishing venture.

She stepped in front of him. "Good morning, Bill. How are you?"

"Good," he said. "Just hoping to catch a few before I start work on the rewiring for the cabins today."

"How many cabins have you rewired?" she asked, crossing her arms over her chest.

"Well, it's been taking longer than I expected. I've done one and a half."

"Bill, Benjamin Hunter recommended you. He

said you would be a good worker. He said you would do good, fair work." She forced herself to stop. She'd heard that remaining silent was an important tool in negotiations. Vivian chewed the inside of her lip and narrowed her eyes. She hoped she looked vicious and intimidating and Bill didn't notice the nervous twitch in her left eye.

"You wouldn't be trying to take advantage of me, would you?" she challenged.

Bill sighed. "No. I wouldn't want to do that." He rubbed his hand across his face. "I don't gotta fish today. I'll work on that next cabin." He paused. "You're not gonna mention this to Ben, are you?"

"Not at the moment," she said, her ire rising at the realization that he might not have responded to her confrontation unless she'd mentioned Benjamin's name. "You do know who is signing your paycheck, writing your future recommendations and allowing you to live rent-free? My name is Vivian Monterey Jackson…"

Bill took a step back and nodded. "Yes, ma'am," he said and headed back to his room, supposedly to get his toolbox so he could get to work on the cabins.

Vivian tried not to grind her teeth, but she couldn't help it. She heard a sound behind her and turned to spot her sister Jilly, who stared at her with a wide-eyed glance.

"You've got balls," Jilly said in wonder.

"I'll take that as a compliment," Vivian said, although she wouldn't trust Bill's performance until he'd made more progress. She was her father's daughter.

That day, she and her sisters worked their butts off painting and completing work on the first cabin. They'd painted the walls a calming spa green and replaced the ratty scatter rugs. A small sitting area with two chairs and a table along with a new microwave, coffeepot and minifridge occupied the side of the room opposite the bed. New shades on the windows would provide a bit of privacy, and new mattresses were on the way for five of the cabins. The other three cabins could wait until they booked some new guests and started making some income again.

"It looks nice. I wouldn't mind staying here, except for the lack of television," Vivian said as the afternoon sun faded from the open blinds.

"You could probably watch some on your iPad by ripping the Wi-Fi from the lodge," Jilly said as if she had experience ripping.

Vivian exchanged a glance with Temple, then brushed her hands together the same way she would have liked to brush aside her concerns about Jilly. After all, her sister was an adult. She'd appeared to survive whatever she'd been doing for the last several years well enough.

"How about we eat an easy dinner, then roast marshmallows and drink wine by the fire pit?" Vivian suggested.

"Can you start a fire from scratch?" Temple asked, her eyes full of doubt.

"I can!" Jilly said with a huge smile on her face. "Didn't you pay attention when Dad showed us?"

"I must confess I haven't had much practice lately," Temple said.

"I can do it. We could roast hot dogs, too."

"Is there anything you can't do?" Temple asked.

Jilly's face fell. "Graduate from college," she said. "Finish just about anything."

Vivian's heart squeezed tight at the lost expression on her youngest sister's face. Silence stretched between the three of them.

"As we're learning, you don't learn everything at college," Temple admitted, even though Vivian and Jilly knew Temple held two advanced degrees. "You can light a fire, and I wouldn't dream of twisting my stiff body into some of those yoga poses you can do. So let's grab those hot dogs, buns and marshmallows." She glanced at Vivian. "A better version of *lunch with the ladies*?"

Vivian smiled and nodded.

Twenty minutes later, the three of them sat around the fire pit as the sun set over the lake. Vivian doused her burned hot dog with mustard and took a bite of it. "Most delicious thing I've eaten in a long time," she said and took another bite.

"Shows how hungry you are," Jilly said. "The more hungry you are, the better anything tastes."

Vivian nodded. "You're probably right. I've eaten some pretty stale sandwiches that tasted good because I skipped lunch." She took a long draw of wine from her red plastic cup. "You know, I was thinking about the last time the three of us were together, and I had a hard time coming up with it."

"Besides your wedding, four and a half years ago at Christmas," Jilly said without batting an eye. She wiped her face with a napkin.

"Too long," Vivian said. "I know Temple has been buried under accounting spreadsheets, and I've been planning events and failing at romance. What have you been doing, Jilly girl?"

"I've been here and there," Jilly said with a shrug. "I went to school to be a massage therapist but skipped the exam. I took a lot of yoga classes, but I had to move before I could finish the teaching preparation. I've tended bar, painted and almost got a cosmetician's license."

Vivian frowned. "You're obviously smart and have super skills. Why didn't you take the exams?"

Jilly shrugged again. "Just didn't ever work out. Anybody want another hot dog? Or are you ready for marshmallows?"

"Marshmallows," Temple said. "And I happened to find an old chocolate bar and some stale graham crackers," she said with a rare jubilant smile as she held up her finds like trophies.

"S'mores," Jilly said. "Oh, wow. With my sisters, eating s'mores by the fire next to the lake. What could be better?"

Vivian still worried about Jilly. It was her nature. She chastised herself for not pressing Jilly for more details during the last few years. She'd been too wrapped up in her own life and making her messes. But for the moment, Jilly was right. What could be better than s'mores with her sisters?

Chapter Four

Vivian made a quick trip to Atlanta to oversee a business conference she'd booked several months ago. She felt guilty leaving her sisters to continue the backbreaking work of refurbishing the cabins. At the same time, Grayson and Millicent were stepping up their game with repairing and cleaning the lodge. Vivian wasn't all that comfortable with Grayson and Millicent working so hard. If they got hurt, she would feel even more guilt. Still, she couldn't boot them out because they didn't have a retirement plan. If she wasn't painting or telecommuting for her full-time job, she was plotting, planning and blogging about the lodge.

Alternately swearing with worry and trying to escape her troubles by singing as she drove back to the lodge, she turned on some music to distract her. She hummed along to her mom's oldies hits and a few eighties songs followed by more recent hits.

By the time she drove up the hill to the lodge, she was in a much better mood. After parking her car, she grabbed her purse and bag, climbed out and headed to the main building.

She mounted the steps and felt a unique sense of home as she entered the foyer. Her life had been chaos for the last several years. How could an old wooden entryway give her such peace?

She took a deep breath and dragged her luggage up the stairway to her room. Sinking onto her bed, she stared at the ceiling. In any other circumstance, she would have wanted, craved, more square foot-age. Somehow, tonight it was enough.

Vivian closed her eyes, ready for some rest.

Her door burst open. Temple stared down with a slightly crazed expression on her face. "Your blog went viral. Everyone wants to have a wedding here."

"What?" Vivian asked, unable to rise from her bed.

"That blog post you wrote last week," Temple said, sitting next to Vivian. "It went viral. Since you left, we've received dozens of requests from people wanting to hold their weddings here."

"Oh, you're joking," Vivian said. She covered her eyes and forehead with her hand. "I posted only three photos, two of the lodge and one of the lake. Tell me you're joking. We're nowhere near ready."

"We need to get ready," Temple said. "This could

mean the difference between making it and not making it."

"That's too much to load on me tonight," Vivian said.

"Okay, okay," Temple said. "But tomorrow morning, we're going to have to work overtime."

"I thought we were already doing that," Vivian said.

"Apparently overtime is relative," Temple said. "But sleep tonight. We will all be begging for sleep soon." She patted Vivian's arm. "Rest well. You'll need it."

Vivian stared at the ceiling. After her insane schedule, she should have been dead asleep. Instead her brain was racing. How had this happened? She'd written the blog post on a friend's site as a test, hoping for feedback. She never would have dreamed so many people would have been interested with so little information. She tried to imagine getting the lodge ready within four weeks, and the prospect nearly made her head explode. She sighed. She wondered if she could possibly sleep with her eyes wide open and her brain so busy.

After she tossed and turned most of the night, Vivian gave up on sleep, took a two-minute shower, dressed and took her laptop and a pad of paper downstairs. It wasn't quite dawn and the lodge was quiet. She got the coffeemaker going and decided to work from the couch on the screened-in porch. The scent of late phlox wafted into the porch, and the sound of the lake lapping at the shore took the edge off her anxiety.

Vivian started out by making a list of the condition of the rooms in the lodge, minimum repairs and upgrades to be made, and then wishful thinking upgrades. Next she began a list of bed-and-breakfasts and the very few decent hotels within thirty miles.

"You're up mighty early," Grayson said from behind her.

Startled, Vivian glanced around to find the elderly man holding two cups of coffee. He offered one to her. "Thank you," she said, accepting the cup.

"I didn't know how you take it, so I added cream and sugar. Seems like most young people don't drink it black," he said and wandered toward the edge of the porch. He looked at the lake. "One of the prettiest sights in the world. Sunrise on the lake from one window. Sunset from another isn't too bad, either."

Vivian took a sip of her coffee and rose from her chair. "It is beautiful," she said.

"Never gets old," he said. "It can get a little dreary in the winter, but the lake makes up for all the gray." He took a few draws of his coffee. "What's got you all bothered this morning, Missy?"

Vivian sighed. "We're going to try to hold more events here at the lodge. I put some information out on the internet, and Temple told me we're already swamped with people asking for information. We're not ready."

"Then tell them that," Grayson said.

Vivian heard an echo of her father in Grayson's

words and felt a twist of missing him. She'd been so busy she hadn't had time to dwell on grief, so it seemed as if the feeling came out of nowhere. She took a slow, deep breath to push aside the tight feeling in her chest.

"It may not be that easy," she said. "If we're going to make the lodge profitable, we need to grab these opportunities."

"Hmm," Grayson said thoughtfully. "One of the things I always respected about your father was that he didn't pretend to be anyone other than who he was, and he didn't promise what he couldn't deliver. This ain't the Biltmore."

Vivian chuckled. "You're right about that. Maybe that's how we should advertise. *Not the Biltmore*."

"I'll be glad to help you with painting and repairs. I'm slower than I used to be, but I'm handy."

Vivian's heart softened at his offer. "You're already doing more than you should."

"Not really," he said. "Millicent and I used to do a lot more, but during the last couple of years, your father wasn't much interested in repairs and improvements."

"Well, I appreciate the offer," she said.

"Millicent and I appreciate having a roof over our heads," he countered. "I see it's your nature to worry, but you and your sisters will make this work. You come from pretty stubborn stock."

"Thanks for the vote of confidence," she said.

She had a powwow with her sisters, but there were too many details to settle before they could put together a brochure with final prices. Instead, each of them selected a room to paint in the lodge. Just after lunchtime, which had been a protein bar and energy drink for her, she heard a loud scream followed by a thump. Another loud wail echoed from down the hall.

Vivian's stomach clenched. That sounded like Millicent. Dropping her paint roller into the pan, she jumped from her ladder and ran down the hall.

"Millicent," she called. "Millicent, is that you?"

"Oh, dear," Millicent cried as Vivian pushed open the door. The woman was crumpled on the floor, holding her leg. "I fell off the chair," she said. "I think I might have broken it."

Vivian rushed to her side. "Oh, no," she said. "Can you move it?"

"I'm afraid to," Millicent said, her face wreathed in pain.

"We need to get you to the doctor," Vivian said.

"What's wrong?" Temple asked from behind her.

"Oh, Millicent," Jilly said, rushing to the old woman's side. She ran her hand gently over Millicent's leg.

"She's afraid to move it," Vivian said.

"She probably shouldn't. Even if she can move it, it can still be broken." Jilly shrugged. "I once temped in a pediatrician's office. We need to get you to the clinic. We just need to figure out a way to transport you from here to the car. I don't think you should hop your way downstairs."

"Should we call an ambulance?" Temple asked.

"That will cost a fortune," Millicent said, shaking her head.

"Insurance will cover it," Vivian assured her.

"Millicent," Grayson said as he entered the room. "What have you done?" He bent down beside her, his hands shaking and his face filled with concern.

"I fell," she said. "The fixtures and curtains needed a good dusting, and like you told me, we need to help these girls as much as possible." Her face crumpled. "And now I'm just causing a heap of trouble."

"Oh, no," Jilly said. "Don't you dare think that. We know you work hard. Right now, we just need to concentrate on getting you treated."

With Jilly's assistance, they reinforced a sun lounger, strapped Millicent into it and carried her downstairs to Temple's SUV. Grayson rode with Temple and Millicent while Vivian and Jilly followed in Vivian's car.

Jilly went into the examination room with Grayson and Millicent because the nurse wouldn't allow all five of them to crowd into the room. Given Jilly's experience, Vivian decided to wait outside. Temple spent the time texting with her firm. After a while, when Millicent was getting X-rays, Vivian took a walk outside.

She paced the sidewalk, worried about Millicent, worried about the lodge, worried about her sisters, worried about everything... She took a deep breath and exhaled. Maybe she should try some yoga, as Jilly had been suggesting.

"Hey, there," a familiar male voice said from behind her.

Benjamin, she thought, her heart beating faster. "Hi," she said, turning around to face him.

"I heard Millicent took a spill," he said. "Is she okay?"

"That news traveled quickly," she said.

"It does around here," he said with an ironic half grin. "So, how is she doing?"

"We're waiting to hear about the X-rays. We were so worried about her when it happened that we all came to the clinic, but the nurse didn't want a crowd in the room during the examination. I can't blame him for that."

Benjamin shook his head. "No. How's everything else going?"

Vivian took in his straightforward gaze and the strength of his shoulders and almost burst into tears. She bit the inside of her cheek, horrified by her reaction. He was just being nice. He didn't want her to fall apart in his arms, even though the prospect was way too inviting.

"It's been a little challenging," she said through a tight throat.

"In what way?" he asked.

"Well, I suddenly feel completely responsible for my sisters and Grayson and Millicent. We've also received interest in booking the lodge for weddings. On the one hand, that's great. On the other hand, I don't want to seize the opportunity too soon, we don't want bad reviews."

"Sounds like a lot," he said. "How can I help?"

She opened her mouth, then closed it. She shouldn't start relying on Benjamin. She suspected it could get addictive, and that wouldn't be good for anyone. "We're okay. Just working it out. I shouldn't have complained."

"Everybody needs a little help now and then," Benjamin said. "Don't be afraid to ask for it."

She took a deep breath. "I don't want to ask too often."

"You sound like your dad."

She shrugged. "That's not all bad, is it?" She tried to shore up her defenses.

He gave a low chuckle that rippled inside her. "I guess not. I'll be in touch, Miss Monterey Aircraft Carrier."

She smiled in return. "Thanks."

She watched him walk away and felt another skip of her heart. Why did he affect her that way?

The good news/bad news was that Millicent's injury was a sprain instead of a break. That said, this sprain required a great deal of recovery time, so everyone in the house would be catering to Millicent.

Vivian and her sisters got back to renovating as well as they could. Jilly kept pushing yoga, and Vivian finally gave in. "Okay, let's do it in the morning," Vivian said. "I'm too tired at the end of the day."

"It would really help in the evening, too," Jilly said.

"So, it won't help in the morning?" Temple asked.

"No, I didn't say that." Jilly nodded. "Let's do mornings." She added under her breath, "It's better than nothing."

Vivian joined in the whole namaste thing for the next several days, despite how distracted she was. As each day passed, she felt more sore. Wasn't she supposed to feel better? Her shoulders were still rising upward in tension.

Tuesday night, she went down to the dock after dark with a glass of wine. She felt achy and discouraged. How was she going to make this work for everyone who was counting on her?

"Vivian," a voice said from behind her. Benjamin.

She glanced over her shoulder as he strode toward her. "What are you doing here?"

"I'm here for the next two weeks," he said. "Your dad gave me a lifetime two-week fishing trip."

"I didn't know that," she said.

"Check his will," he said and sat down next to her. "I could be helpful. I'm decently handy."

Benjamin popped open a beer and offered her the same.

"I'm sipping my wine," she said.

"I'll bring wine next time," he said.

"No need," she said. "There won't be a next time."

"Don't say that," he said. "Anything can happen."

"That's what I thought when I was a teenager," she said. "I tried to get you to join me in the lake, but you said no."

"Well, now I'm saying yes."

Her heart skipped a beat, but she ignored it. "It's a little late."

"Think about it," he said.

She glanced at his too-appealing half grin and strong body. Broad shoulders, muscular arms and lean hips. He had aged quite well. Why was she noticing his body? she asked herself. She needed to ignore it.

"No need," she said and rose.

Vivian successfully avoided Benjamin the next night, but she couldn't stay away from the dock too long. After dark two nights later, she carried her glass of wine to sit and sip under the stars.

Despite Jilly's best efforts, Vivian found evenings on the dock more therapeutic than anything. Hearing heavy steps on the dock, she braced herself. It had to be Benjamin.

Without saying a word, he sat down beside her, his legs hanging over the edge of the dock. He put an open bottle of wine between them.

Vivian picked it up and studied the bottle. "It's white. Well done."

"Good to know. I thought I noticed you preferred white."

She poured a half glass. "I can't drink this whole bottle."

"You could try," he said with a grin.

"You are bad," she said.

"In a good way," he returned. "Wanna go for a swim?"

"No," she said immediately. "It's too cold."

"I could keep you warm," he suggested.

"Why couldn't you have said this when I was fifteen?" she asked.

"Your father would have killed me," he said.

"Coward," she said.

He met her gaze for a long moment. "You're calling me a coward?"

"You turned me down all those years ago," she told him.

"You need to look at the overall picture. I was respecting your father."

"And now?" she asked.

"Now I'm going to get you," he said, lowering his head to hers. "In every way."

Her heart spiked. "Oh, I don't think so. I'm older and wiser."

"But you still feel it between you and me, don't you?" he asked. "It hasn't gone away, has it?"

Vivian frowned at him. "There's a remnant. I'm sure it will go away soon." She grabbed the bottle of wine and stood. "You're a little too cocky for my taste."

Benjamin laughed, and the sound was lusty and full of life. She wished she could laugh that way. "You like your men cocky. You always have," he said as she tramped down the dock, her peace totally destroyed by her interaction with him.

She sighed. He needed to go away. She should check her father's will.

"Hey, Viv, don't forget I'm at the end of the hall on the second floor. You have an open invitation."

Chapter Five

Vivian did some number-crunching in her bedroom. She played HGTV in the background, but watching how all the fix-it people seemed to repair everything at the speed of light made her feel more frustrated.

A knock sounded at her door. "Don't be Benjamin," she whispered under her breath. Then she called, "Who is it?"

"Temple. Let me in. Why is your door—"

Vivian opened the door.

"—locked," Temple finished and studied her. "You look cranky. What's wrong? Are the numbers worse than we thought?"

"Not really. I just wish we had one of those

HGTV teams where they come in and fix everything overnight."

Temple shot her a skeptical look. "I'm not sure how long-lasting those overnight jobs are. But we're not doing badly, and now that Benjamin has shown up, things are moving even more quickly. He's a real workhorse."

Vivian frowned. "He wouldn't be here if he hadn't made that arrangement with Daddy."

"Well, maybe we should extend it. The electrician is really starting to hustle, and the part-time plumber is hanging in longer than part-time. Everybody likes Benjamin. He seems to inspire people, and you used to have a big crush on him."

"That was fifteen years ago," Vivian said. "He's just so cocky."

"Aren't most football players? He used to play football, didn't he?" Temple asked.

"Quarterback," Vivian said. "They make the calls."

"I didn't know you watched football," Temple said.

"With Daddy," Vivian said. "I covered football. You talked basketball."

Temple stared at her for a long moment and shifted her glasses, then gave her a sad smile. "We sure tried to fill that son vacancy, didn't we?"

Vivian's throat tightened, but she managed to choke out a laugh. "I still say Jilly pulled it off the best."

"Is there anything she can't do, at least partly?"

"Maybe read well," Vivian said in a low voice. "I

remember Mom taking her for some special lessons. It seemed like she was always frustrated with her."

"I've been so focused on becoming a partner with my firm," Temple said. "I'm not sure what all happened between Mom and her."

"I know what you're saying. I worry about what she has gone through. I asked Mom about it one time and she cut me off at the knees." She paused and took a breath. "I want to take better care of Jilly."

"Even though it looks like she's done a pretty good job taking care of herself?" Temple asked.

"Yeah. I don't want her to have to take odd jobs just to survive. She deserves better than that," Vivian said.

Temple lightly touched her arms. "Careful. You're turning into a mother hen."

"How can I not? Between Grayson, Millicent, Jilly and you putting your life savings on the line…"

"Well, not my whole life savings." Temple adjusted her glasses again. "I'm not that naive. We'll get through this. We each have our own talents. Do yoga. Go to sleep. Can I get you some wine?"

"No. I'm fine."

"You are doing fine," Temple said and put her arms around Vivian in an awkward hug.

"I think I'll take a bath," Vivian said.

"Good idea. Trust me, the numbers will always be there whether you're dead or alive."

"Yeah. Thanks. I guess," Vivian said and mustered a smile. "I'll be better in the morning."

"Sure you will. Jilly will get you all twisted with

yoga," Temple said. "Get some rest, princess. You've always been the working kind of princess."

Vivian stared after her sister as she left the room. She and her sisters had often been so busy surviving that they hadn't had much time for each other. Vivian had tried to keep everyone happy and often felt as if she'd failed. Temple had been brainy, but not all that sociable. They'd both been shuttled off to boarding school at a relatively young age. Jilly had been sent off, too, but she hadn't fit in. She'd struggled. Even now, Vivian wished she'd paid better attention. Maybe things would have turned out easier for Jilly...

Vivian's head throbbed, and she squeezed her temples. Time for a bath and some jazz music to push down her porcupine quills. After turning on the taps to the tub, she grabbed her iPod and stripped off her clothes. Stepping into the tub, she sank into the water up to her chin and focused on the music. The water caressed her skin, reminding her of how little she'd been touched lately. She should get a massage, she told herself, but as the water lapped over her nipples and warmed her all over, her mind wandered to Benjamin. How would his big hands feel on her body? Would he be rough or tender? How would his hard, muscled body feel against hers?

She wriggled in the water, feeling an aching awareness in places she hadn't paid any attention to lately. The jazz music seeped throughout her and she tried not to think about Benjamin, but want grew inside her. She tried to push it aside, yet even after she dried off and went to bed, she couldn't stop thinking about his invitation. If she went to his room, maybe he could ease the ache inside her, and she could get on with what she needed to do.

Vivian knew she wouldn't. She was ashamed to admit even to herself that she didn't have the nerve.

The next morning, she focused on sun salutations with Jilly. The poses were killing her. "Jilly, I don't know about this downward dog. I'm having a hard time with it. Jet doesn't ever do this kind of stuff," Vivian said. "He just stays conked out on that rug in the bar."

"Shh," Jilly said. "Just breathe and give in to the stretch."

"I'm not really feeling the Zen," Vivian said.

Jilly sighed. "That's not a problem. Let's do child's pose. That should help."

Vivian gratefully sank onto her mat. This was one pose she could actually say she loved. "Can I stay this way all day?"

Jilly laughed. "No, but let's do a little meditation."

Vivian rose and tried to focus on Jilly's words, but her mind grew busy. There were too many things to do today and tomorrow. There were too many things that needed to turn out just right. Her body stiffened.

"You're not paying attention," Jilly said. "I can feel it."

"Why do you have to be so perceptive?" Vivian asked. "Stop it."

Jilly chuckled. "We all have our skills. We'll try again tomorrow."

"If we must," Vivian said as she hobbled to her feet. She gave her sister a squeeze. "Thanks, beautiful."

Vivian headed out of the screened-in porch while Jilly worked on harder poses. She brushed her hand over her forehead and nearly walked straight into Benjamin's hard chest. "Oh, my. I didn't see you. Um, good morning," she said and noticed he was carrying two fishing rods.

"Good morning to you," he said, pulling his ball cap into place. "You're just who I was looking for."

Vivian blinked. "Why?"

"So we can go fishing," he said. "Two poles. I'll even bait your hook for you."

"I don't have time to go fishing," she said. "But thank you."

"It won't take long," he said. "It'll do more for you than that yoga with your sister."

"I find that hard to believe," she said.

"You're not sore?" he asked.

"Yes, but that's part of the process," she said.

"I can guarantee you won't get sore from fishing," he said.

"If I don't slice my fingers to ribbons trying to put a worm on the hook," she grumbled.

"I already said I'd do that for you. C'mon. I'll just keep you an hour. If you don't feel better after an hour, then I won't make you do it again."

Make her, she thought. He wouldn't make her do

anything. At the same time, she wondered if it might help her to spend a little time on the lake. "Just an hour," she said, relenting. "I have work to do."

"So do I, but I'll get more done if I start out this way," he said. "Maybe you will, too."

She was skeptical, but something in his gaze offered a temporary escape she wanted or needed. But she wouldn't confess to that. Never. Ever.

Benjamin watched Vivian, sitting in the boat across from him, eyeing the hook with trepidation. She was a girlie-girl who'd always tried her best to be more sporty, probably to please her father, and that was one of the reasons she'd always fascinated him. She was willing to step out of her comfort zone.

Benjamin felt her watching him bait his hook.

"I should at least try," she said.

He put his hand over hers. "Not this time."

"Why?" she asked. "You're so sure I can't do it."

"No," he said. "I just don't want this to be the last time you go fishing with me. One thing at a time. I bet you're good at casting." Casting was like shifting gears. Once you got out of Neutral, you were in good shape. He put a juicy worm on her hook. "Show me your stuff."

She looked at the rod, then at him. "This is embarrassing. I've forgotten how. I never dated a fisherman," she said, clearly exasperated.

"That's your first problem," he said. "It will all come back to you. Use your thumb to hold down the casting reel. Pull it back, then slide it forward and release." He nodded as she followed his instructions. "There you go. Perfect."

"I've never been called perfect," she muttered.

"Then maybe you've been hanging around the wrong people," he said.

Her head snapped up and she met his gaze. She might have been raised in Virginia, but her eyes were Carolina blue. He felt the intense, deeper-than-it-should-have-been connection ricochet between them.

She must have felt it, too, because she looked away. "When are you going to cast yours?" she asked, not meeting his gaze.

"Right now," he said and cast his line over the other side of the boat.

After several moments, she sighed and shrugged her shoulders. "I'm remembering why I didn't love fishing. It takes so long."

"Relax. Take a deep breath. This is your opportunity to slow down."

"I don't have time to slow down," she said. "I need to paint a bathroom."

"You'll do it faster if you fish first. Trust me," he said. "Stop thinking about everything you think you need to do and listen to the lake."

Vivian took a deep breath. A thousand thoughts tried to storm through her mind, but she deliberately pushed them aside. She focused on the sounds of the lake. A bird called in the distance. The water made gentle swishing sounds. Gradually she felt soothed. Just a bit.

Something tugged on her line, and she nearly jumped out of her skin. "Ohmygoodness, I have a bite."

"Good for you. Just hold on. Reel him in," he coached.

Benjamin could feel her concentration. Moments later, she pulled the squirming fish into the boat.

"Oh, no," she said. "Look what I've done. I've killed a fish. Should I throw him back in?"

Benjamin bit his lip. "No. You're going to eat him."

Vivian made a face. "Oh, I don't know."

"I will fix him up for you. He's your trophy meal. You deserve it."

"What about the worm?"

"I'll get rid of the worm," he told her and put the fish in the ice chest. "Can you relax now?"

"I'm not sure," she said. "My heart is racing and I feel like I should be doing something."

"You should," he said. "You should be kissing me."

She shot him a suspicious glance.

"Kiss me," he said. "You'll feel better. I promise."

"You're ridiculous," she said, but after a moment, she leaned forward and pressed her mouth against his.

Benjamin slid his hand behind her neck and took her mouth, deepening the kiss. She tasted sweet, like the girl he'd always wanted but never gotten. The boat began to rock. He reached out one of his hands to steady her, but she pulled back.

"I think that's enough," she said breathlessly.

"Do you really?" he asked, leaning toward her.

Vivian leaned backward. "I do," she said.

Benjamin felt a tug on his line and pulled in the fish. "Dinner for two," he said.

"You can have mine," she said.

He shook his head. "Didn't your daddy tell you that you're supposed to eat what you catch?"

"I guess," she said. "What if I don't like this kind of fish?"

"You will," he said. "I'll use the kitchen at the lodge. We can meet on the dock this afternoon."

"I'm not sure it's a good idea," she said. "You're very distracting."

"Thank you," he said.

After her fishing expedition, Vivian painted a bathroom and a quarter of a bedroom. By the end of the day, she ached from head to toe. "All I want is pain meds and my bed," she said as she slumped down in the hall and took a long sip from her water bottle.

Jilly joined her. "Yoga would help," she told her.

Vivian winced and shook her head. "I don't think so. I've been sore every day since I've been doing yoga."

Jilly pursed her lips. "Maybe I've overestimated you. Maybe you need yoga for older people."

Vivian glanced at her sister, insulted. "Excuse me. I'm not old."

"Well, you're not old," Jilly corrected herself.

"But you're new, and you haven't stretched much. The older you get..."

Vivian gave her sister the death glare. "Don't call me old."

Temple hobbled down the hallway toward them. "I need a pain reliever. Maybe something stronger than over-the-counter."

"You and me both," Vivian said.

"I think the lodge would benefit from a spa," Jilly said. "Especially since many older people will visit."

Temple and Vivian glared at her.

Jilly shrugged. "Tell me you wouldn't benefit from soaking in a Jacuzzi. Maybe we should get more than one."

"Because we have so much extra money," Vivian said.

"I bet it's not that much extra," Jilly said.

Temple cocked her head to one side. "You might be right. We should think about it."

"Really, Miss Penny Pincher?" Vivian asked Temple.

"Yeah," Temple said. "They are not hideously expensive, and they evoke luxury."

"Inside or outside?" Vivian asked.

"Outside. That way we can skip indoor mold," Temple said.

"Can we put up a sign that tells people not to pee in the spa?" Vivian asked.

Jilly giggled.

"We can," Temple said. "But we can't skip chlorine."

"Just think how much you could be relaxing in a Jacuzzi right now," Jilly said.

Vivian closed her eyes and groaned. "I wonder how quickly we can get them."

Hearing heavy steps walking toward them on the hallway, she glanced up to see Benjamin. Her heart skipped over itself.

"Fish is ready. I don't want it to get cold. Come on down to the dock," he said.

"I need a shower," she protested.

"Jump in the lake," he said. "I'm hungry."

Vivian scrambled to her feet and stared after him as he walked toward the stairs.

"You went fishing?" Temple asked more than said.

"It was a dare," Vivian said.

"Hmm," Temple said in disbelief.

"Fishing," Jilly said with a mischievous smile. "You'll have to tell us all about it. Go ahead, now, and enjoy…it all."

"I couldn't turn him down," Vivian said. "He said I only had to do it once."

"Sounds like it went well," Temple said.

Vivian groaned. "Stop it. Stop it. Stop it."

"Bet that fish is gonna be delicious," Jilly said. "And maybe the man, too."

Chapter Six

Benjamin successfully seduced her—into joining him in eating their catch of the day with some great sides.

With her honey-blond hair in a ponytail and her face clean except for a few swipes of paint, Vivian looked almost the same as she had fifteen years ago. Except for her curves. She'd definitely filled out in that department. He'd told himself she wasn't his type, but he couldn't resist the urge to get to know her better. Maybe if he spent some time with her, he wouldn't find her such a source of temptation.

"Hush puppies, fried fish and French fries," she said as Benjamin gave her a full plate. "If I die from this, I'm sending my sisters after you."

"There are cabbage and carrots in the coleslaw.

That counts as a vegetable," he said, sitting beside her on the dock. "If you don't want it—"

"Don't even think about taking away this food now that you've tempted me with it." She took a bite of a hush puppy and moaned in approval. "Did you make all of this?"

"No. Grayson did most of it. He also warned me not to take advantage of Jedediah's daughter."

She slid a sideways glance at him. "I'm sure you'll heed his wise words."

Benjamin chuckled at her sly glance. "You're well past the age of consent."

"Are you calling me old?" she countered with a scowl.

"Not at all. If I didn't know better, I'd probably card you at my bar."

Appearing mollified, she twitched her lips. "Well, I'll take that as a compliment," she said and took a bite of fried fish. "Delicious."

"When was the last time you caught your own dinner?" he asked.

"A very long time ago. My dad insisted I bait my own hook, and I was squeamish about it. That meant I spent a lot of time watching and reading."

"Reading?" he said.

She nodded. "He allowed me to bring a book. Otherwise, he said I talked too much and would disturb the fish. I think my chatter bothered him a lot more than it bothered the fish."

"Probably so. I don't think he always knew what to do with three girls."

"I think he tried hard to counter my mom's influence. Ballet, piano, private school, finishing school."

"You think he was successful?" Benjamin asked.

Vivian sighed. "Depends on the day. I know I made some choices due to my mother's expectations. I remember my wedding day. Daddy and I were just getting ready to walk down the aisle. He had never trusted Robert. Daddy turned to me and said, 'You can still call it off. I've got the keys to my Jeep in my pocket.'" She gave a wry smile. "I still remember hearing the jingle of his keys over the sound of Canon in D by Pachelbel."

"And what did you say?"

"'Mom would die.'" Her lips twitched. "He said, 'Mom doesn't have to sleep with him.' He used other, more colorful language, but you catch my drift."

"I guess he had a point," Benjamin said and chuckled.

"In retrospect, he did, but I was hoping things would turn out different." She took another bite of hush puppy and glanced about him. "No temptations to walk down the aisle for you?"

"Once, but it just wasn't right," he said. "No regrets. It turned out for the best for everybody."

"You never missed her?" Vivian asked.

He shrugged. "Maybe once or twice. I had other things to do. What about you? Do you miss your ex?"

"For a while, I missed the man I'd hoped he was, but he wasn't that man. The bad thing is, it made me lose my trust in myself. You need to look at people for who they are, not who you want them to be."

"True, but some of us make a few improvements along the way. If we're determined. And lucky."

"Maybe so," she said. "I didn't realize how profound you could be."

"You just thought I was all good looks and muscle," he said and winked at her.

"I knew you were smart, too," she protested. "I already told you I was surprised you didn't go pro and never look back at the town."

"There are times when you have to step up. That was one of those times. But enough about me. I see you've cleaned your plate."

"Yes, I did. Shame on you," she said with a sexy little pout. "I'll have to run up and down the mountain for three days to work that off."

"You're doing plenty of labor. How about a swim?" he asked, picking up the paper plates and taking them to the trash can.

"I'm not wearing a bathing suit," she said.

"So?" he asked.

"It's still daylight," she told him. "I'm not swimming in the nude in broad daylight."

"The sun will set soon enough. Meet me here at eight thirty. I'll bring some wine. You can even wear a swimsuit if you're a scaredy-cat."

"The water is too cold. I won't be goaded into skinny-dipping," she said.

"I'm not goading," he told her, extending his hand to her. "I'm just teasing a little."

She shot him a distrustful glance, but accepted his hand and stood. He stared into her crystal-blue eyes and took in her creamy skin and inviting pink lips. Her T-shirt and jeans were casual, but he couldn't help noticing the way her breasts stretched the gray cotton, and there was no denying the curve of her hips in the denim.

Benjamin sighed and lifted his hand to her chin. Vivian's eyes widened slightly, but she didn't pull back. "I wouldn't have ever thought you'd get any prettier than you were when you were a teenager. But you've grown into yourself. You've turned into a beautiful woman, a smart one, too, with a good heart. Your father would kill me for what I'm thinking right now."

Vivian swallowed and her eyelids fluttered downward, hiding her expression from him. "I guess it's a good thing he doesn't know."

"I guess so," Benjamin said. "I've got to make a quick trip into town. Don't forget. Eight thirty here at the dock," he said and headed up the hill.

"I didn't say I was coming," she called after him.

"Eight thirty," he said over his shoulder and grinned to himself. He was going to reel this little beauty in, and she wouldn't have any idea what hit her. He'd make sure of it.

She should just paint another room, Vivian told herself as she eyed the clock. Eight twenty-five. Or indulge in a television binge like Jilly. Or do some paperwork like Temple. None of the prospects appealed to her.

A bath, she suggested to herself. A nice, long bath, read a book, then go to sleep. That would be the best therapy in the world for her since her body was aching and her mind needed to settle down.

Vivian glanced at the clock again. Eight twenty-eight. Shutting down a dozen objections and warnings, she grabbed her swimsuit and jerked it on, then snagged a towel and flew out the door. Benjamin would mock her for the suit, but maybe a dip in lake water would do her some good. Oh, who was she fooling? She just wanted to see him again.

He stood on the dock and lifted the wineglasses as he watched her make her way toward him. She felt his gaze on her every step of the way, and it gave her a little thrill.

"Two glasses," she said, accepting one. "You must have been confident I would join you."

"I'd like to put your presence down to my irresistible manly charms. But you've come down to the dock more evenings than not," he said. "However, this time you're wearing a bathing suit. If I can get you in the water…"

"Don't count on anything else," she said.

He took a deep sip of his wine and set his glass on the dock, then pulled off his T-shirt. "Don't worry."

Then he proceeded to shuck his shorts and underwear with his pretty amazing backside to her and jumped in the lake.

Vivian choked on her wine. He bobbed to the surface and waved for her to join him.

"I thought I'd take it slow—sit down and dip in my feet, slide in a little bit at a time," she said.

"That'll take all night," he said. "Jump in all at once. That's the way to go."

"It must be freezing," she said, suspicious.

"It's not freezing. I would be turning blue if it were," he assured her. He lifted his hands. "Come on, Vivian. I'll catch you."

His words made something inside her soften. Since getting divorced over three years ago, she'd been hesitant in her relationships. She'd wondered if someone was going to pull the rug out from beneath her when she least expected it. Benjamin might be a charmer, but she suspected he meant it when he said he'd catch her.

After taking a couple of big gulps of wine, she set down the glass beside her towel, walked to the end of the dock and jumped. The temperature of the water shocked her down to her bones. She gasped at the cold that not even Benjamin's arms could conceal.

"You lied," she said to Benjamin. "It's freezing."

"Refreshing," he corrected her.

"Freezing," she said, shaking her head.

"All right, it's a little brisk, but I'll warm you up," he said and tugged her along as he swam farther into the lake. "Tell the truth—this is nice. It's quiet and peaceful, with stars up above."

"I'll tell you when I regain sensation. At the moment, I'm still numb from the cold."

"Ah, so you're cranky when you get a little chilly," he said. "I'll have to remember that."

"It's more than a little chilly," she retorted, but his arms did feel nice, and his shoulders were so broad and strong. She took a deep breath and sighed. She might as well enjoy the moment.

"Listen," he said. "Close your eyes and listen."

Vivian did as he asked and heard the sound of a bird. "What kind?" she asked.

"Whip-poor-will."

She opened her eyes and looked at him. With his tousled wet hair and drops of lake water on his face, he was ridiculously appealing to her. It was almost a sin for a man to be so sexy. There should have been something wrong with him. She should focus on finding out what that horrible quality was.

"Stop thinking," he told her and spun her around in the water.

She laughed at the combination of his words and the sensation of spinning. "How do you know I'm thinking?"

"Your eyebrows pull down and you stop smiling," he said and spun her around again.

"This is nicer than I thought it was going to be," she said.

"I could make it a lot nicer," he suggested.

She gave him a sideways glance, but he lowered his head anyway and pressed his mouth against hers. She had the sensation of spinning even though she knew the only movement Benjamin made besides kissing and holding her was kicking his legs to keep them above water. He felt so good, so strong, so delicious. Her heart hammered in her chest, and she kissed him back. She wanted more.

His tongue slid over hers, and she noticed the way his strong chest felt against her breasts. Lower, she felt him between her legs. She couldn't resist pressing against him.

He made a low groan that vibrated in her mouth and throughout her body. "I think we should get rid of this swimsuit," he said.

"Hmm," she said, wanting more of his kisses, wanting not to think. She took his mouth again and indulged herself with his lips. A few seconds later, he pulled off her bathing suit top tossed it on the dock, and she felt her bare nipples, taut and achy, rubbing against his chest.

He took one of her breasts in his hand. "So pretty," he said and rubbed her nipple. "You feel so good." He removed her bottoms and lifted her hips, urging her to straddle him, making her aware of his arousal.

Even though a combination of adrenaline and desire was raging through her, Vivian's brain still worked. Sex in the lake? What if someone saw them? What about protection? What about— "I don't think this is a good idea," she managed breathlessly, tugging her mouth from his.

"Really?" he asked. "Why not? We're adults."

The look in his eyes made her mouth go dry. "Yes, but protection," she said.

"Got it," he said.

"What if someone sees us?"

"Not likely, but we can go to my room. Or yours." He paused and gave a pained chuckle. "Unless you're getting cold feet."

"It's not cold feet," she said, then sighed. "Well, maybe a little. You're just a lot of—" She broke off, thinking, *You're just a lot of man.*

"That's bad?"

"No," she said. "I'm not sure how to handle you."

"I can help you figure that out," he said. "But no pressure. If you don't want to go further, we won't."

A big part of her really wanted to go further. Conflicted, she bit her lip. "Okay. Thanks."

He swam back to the dock, pulling her along with him, and lifted her to the dock, following after her. He returned the top of her swimsuit to her. Embarrassed because she'd forgotten about it, she struggled to tie it.

"I can help," he said and took care of the task with steady hands.

Vivian climbed the ladder, darted for her towel and trained her gaze on the shore, away from Benjamin. She heard his feet on the dock as he put on his clothes. At least, she hoped he was getting dressed. She felt his hand on her shoulder and jumped.

"It's safe. You can look now," he said with a twinge of humor.

Vivian rolled her eyes, mostly at herself. She collected her wineglass and headed toward the house.

"No need to rush off," he said.

She thought about denying that she was hurrying

away, then decided it was time to be a grown-up. Turning around, she met his gaze. "I need to clear my head. You have muddled it."

"I think that's one of the nicest things I've ever been told," he said. "See you tomorrow night on the dock."

"I don't know."

"We can talk," he said. "Or I can kiss you all night long. It might drive us both wild, but we will enjoy the ride." He leaned toward her and brushed his mouth against her cheek. The caress made her feel weak all over again.

"'Night, Viv," he said.

"G'night, Benjamin," she said and stiffened her legs and her backbone. Lord help her, that man was distracting.

Vivian tossed and turned again that night. In the wee hours, she wondered again if she should just go ahead and share a night with Benjamin to get him out of her system. At the same time, she wasn't at all sure the one-time tactic would work. But realistically, could he be that good?

By midmorning, she heard a hound dog howling in the distance. The mournful sound wafted through the open window, tugging at her heartstrings. She heard a few more howls and suddenly realized it was Jet.

She went into the hallway. Grayson appeared. "Jet?" she asked.

He nodded. "He sounds like he's in trouble. I'll

go look for him, but someone needs to stay with Millicent."

"No. I'll go. I just need you to tell me where you think he might be."

"Neighbor's property. He got stuck in a barbed fence one other time. I hope he didn't get into that again."

"Should I drive?"

"You'll have better luck walking. It's past the cabins. You sure you don't want me to go?" he asked, clearly worried.

"No. I'll leave right now," she said and wondered why neither of her sisters had heard the howling. Checking in on Jilly, she saw her sister moving her head in rhythm to whatever music she was playing on her iPod as she painted a guest room.

Vivian moved in front of her sister and waved her arms. Jilly removed her earbuds. "What up?"

"Jet ran off. He's howling, so we're afraid he's hurt himself."

"Oh, no," Jilly said, crestfallen. Jilly was so tenderhearted about animals. "We need to find him."

Vivian nodded. "I'll get Temple. Grayson says Jet's wails sound like they are coming from the neighboring property. Take your cell phone so we can stay in touch."

Vivian also found Temple painting and wearing earbuds. She was told Temple had been listening to a podcast on corporate accounting. All three of them ran to the path past the cabins. As they approached the barbed wire fence, Vivian listened for Jet. "No howls," she said.

"I'm not sure whether that's a good thing or a bad thing," Temple said. "And how are we supposed to get over that fence without ripping ourselves to shreds?"

Vivian pulled off her sweatshirt. It was a chilly morning, so she was wearing a tank top underneath. "I'll donate my shirt to the cause. Unless we hear more from Jet, I think we need to split up to find him. Just keep your cell phone ready."

"Even though the coverage up here may not be stellar," Temple said, making the first move over the fence.

"Let's just do our best," Vivian muttered as she watched Jilly tackle the fence next.

Vivian followed, then headed up the hill. Since Jet hated baths, he could be stinky. She wondered if she could smell him if she couldn't hear him. Climbing through the woods and leaves, she thought she heard the soft sound of a whine, but she wasn't sure if she'd imagined it. She moved in the direction of the sound. Breathless from rushing and climbing, she stepped over a series of fallen trees and branches and came upon Jet, whining, and Benjamin standing over the dog with his hands on his hips.

Relief flooded through her as she walked toward them. "Is he okay?"

"Not sure. He stepped into a trap. Looks like his leg is in bad shape."

Jet gave a miserable little whine that tore at her.

She put her hand on his head, and he turned to lick it as if he were saying, *Please help me.* "How do we get him out?"

"Without wire cutters, it's a two-person job," he said. "I've got a rope to fasten to Jet's collar so he won't run away. Not that he'll be able to move too fast. I'll hook it to my belt. Then I'll pull this side of the trap, and you pull the other. If you think you can," he added.

"Of course I can," she said, at the same time wishing she'd done a little more strength training lately. Ideally all that painting would help.

"Okay. You may have to hold your side for thirty seconds. Warn me if you're about to let it go," he said.

"I will. I will," she said and put her hands on one side of the steel trap, frowning at the unforgiving metal teeth. "I hate these things," she muttered. "If they're not catching snakes, they should be outlawed."

"Countdown to pulling," he said. "Three. Two. One."

Vivian struggled to hold her side. Using all her strength, she was appalled to see that she'd separated her side by mere inches.

"It's okay. Almost got him," Benjamin said, holding one end of his side with his foot. He carefully pulled Jet's paw free. The dog yelped and hobbled to a few feet away. "You can let go now," Benjamin said. "Good job."

Vivian let out the breath of air she'd been holding. Sweat trickled between her breasts and she had the oddest urge to cry.

Benjamin was checking Jet's paw as much as the dog would allow. Vivian stepped closer. She saw quite a bit of matted fur and blood. "How bad is it?"

"I don't know. He might lose the paw. We need to get him to the vet."

"I'll call Temple and Jilly."

Her sisters met them at the bottom of the hill. "All of us don't need to go to the vet," Vivian said. "I'd like you two to stay at the house." If something worse happened to Jet, then she wanted to soften the blow for her sisters.

Jilly pouted. "But what if something goes wrong with him?"

"I'll call you. I promise," Vivian said.

Temple gave Jet a quick pat on the head, but Jilly hugged him as if her and his lives depended on it. When she pulled back, she had tears in her eyes.

Vivian hugged her sister. "Go tell Grayson we found Jet and we're taking him to the veterinarian. I'll call you as soon as we know anything."

Jilly nodded. "Thanks, Benjamin."

"Glad I could help. We should get going," he said.

Vivian and Benjamin walked quickly to his SUV. When Benjamin started to put Jet in the back, Vivian stopped him. "Don't you think I should hold him?"

"I thought he would be more comfortable back here," he said.

"If you're sure. Maybe I could ride back there with him," she said and climbed in with the dog.

Benjamin gave a slow nod, then got into the cab and drove into town. Memories of her father and Jet filled Vivian's mind during the drive. Jet had enjoyed going hunting with her dad, but he'd hated being bathed. Her father had insisted and always won the battle. She remembered watching Jet riding in a fishing boat with her father. Her father had loved that dog, and the dog had returned the affection.

Jet had stayed with her father even at the end. The dog wouldn't leave Jedediah's side. At that moment, it struck her that Jet had been the only living being with her father when he died at home. He'd kept the seriousness of his illness from almost everyone. A knot formed in her throat. Vivian stroked Jet's head and chest. The dog closed his eyes as if he appreciated the comfort. It was the least she could do. Jet had been so loyal to her father throughout the years.

She remembered the first summer she'd met the dog. He'd sniffed her and occasionally allowed her to pet him, but he clearly wasn't all that interested in her. Jedediah had been his sole focus.

Jet whined and it tore at her. She and the dog might not have been best buddies, but she didn't want him to die. Suddenly her eyes filled with tears and her chest hurt so badly.

Benjamin pulled to a stop beside the animal hospital. Vivian willed herself to dry her tears. She swiped at her cheeks with the backs of her hands, but she couldn't stop herself.

When Benjamin opened the door, she wanted to hide her face.

"Aw, sweetheart. Come here," he said and pulled her into his embrace.

"I don't understand why I can't stop crying. That dog doesn't even like me very much. And he stinks," she added, sobbing.

"He's a part of your dad you don't want to lose," Benjamin said.

"Kinda like the lodge. And Millicent. And Grayson." She sniffed. "When am I going to stop chasing him when I know he's gone?"

"Nah, he's not gone. There are pieces of Jedediah all over the place. In your sisters. In Jet. You just want as much as you can get. No shame in that."

Vivian felt something inside her crack open just a little bit. It was both a relief and scary at the same time. This whole thing was getting to her. Benjamin was getting to her. Being with him made her feel both exhilarated and at peace. She'd never felt this way about a man and it was becoming more and more difficult to keep her heart safe from him.

Chapter Seven

Jet's paw was shredded from the trap, but the vet seemed hopeful that he would recover. "He just needs to rest and keep the bandage clean," Vivian repeated the vet's instructions under her breath as Benjamin pulled into the driveway to the lodge.

"He spends most every day in a half coma. What got into him today?" she muttered, petting Jet's head.

"A full moon is coming. That can make any creature act weirdly," Benjamin said.

She nodded, wondering if the moon was causing her to act out of character. "The vet looked at me strangely when I asked if he wouldn't mind giving Jet a bath today."

"They just want to wait a day for his wound to

heal a little. Jedediah would turn in in his grave if he thought you were going to pay to get Jet washed. He always did it with the hose."

"I've been thinking about that. Maybe Jet wouldn't hate getting cleaned as much if the water was warmer and the experience wasn't so unpleasant."

"Are you talking about a spa day for Jet?" Benjamin asked doubtfully, glancing at her in the rearview mirror.

"Hey, it's worth a try. Until then, we'll use this doggy deodorant I bought from the vet."

"Bet Jet will lick it off," Benjamin said, pulling the SUV to a stop. He rounded to the back and opened the hatch. "I'm surprised you haven't said a word about the vet bill."

"I'm still in shock," she said. "But I was so afraid he wouldn't be okay that I was all, 'Here, take my money.'" She shook her head and looked down at the hound. "You're worth every stinkin' cent, aren't you, Jet?"

The dog licked her hand as if to thank her.

"Looks like he's starting to like you," Benjamin said, helping her out of the back of the SUV.

"Gold diggin' sweetie pie," she said, rubbing the dog again. She turned to look up at Benjamin. "Thank you for everything."

"Does this mean I get an extra day of fishing?"

"You can have an extra week. I was a wreck," she said. "I sure couldn't have released him from the jaws of that trap by myself."

Benjamin put his arm around her. "I think you

did pretty well. I'll have a word with your neighbor, although he's allowed to set traps on his property."

Jilly and Temple burst out the door. "Is he okay? How's his paw?"

"We both want to see for ourselves," Jilly said and rushed to pat Jet.

"True," Temple said. "Bet it wasn't cheap."

Vivian lifted her eyebrows at her sister. "Are you saying I should have refused service?"

"Oh, no," Temple said, then lifted her hands. "But I'm an accountant, so I think about this stuff."

"I understand. I think we may need to keep Jet on a leash for a while," Vivian said.

"Leash?" Benjamin echoed. "I don't think Jedediah ever put Jet on a leash."

"No baths, no leash," Vivian said. "This is getting better and better."

She glanced at Benjamin and saw him frown as he read something on his cell phone. "Problem?" she asked.

"I need to go back into town," he said. "I'll carry Jet up to his dog bed, and then I need to leave."

Just like that, Benjamin's whole demeanor changed. He was distracted and unhappy. She wondered what was bothering him so much. She wished he would tell her, but she could see he was shut down tight.

Benjamin pushed the speed limit on the way to the pharmacy in town. Damn insurance. His sister had a hard enough time staying on her medication without the insurance company making it difficult for her.

He pushed open the door to the drugstore and saw his sister squared off with the man at the cash register. "Miss Hunter, it says here that your insurance will not cover this medication. I'm sorry, but—"

"That's a crock," Eliza said. "Why would my doctor prescribe something my insurance wouldn't cover?"

"Doctors don't always keep track of all the rules with insurance. Nowadays it's nearly impossible," the pharmacist told her and adjusted his glasses.

"Well, I can't pay that much," she yelled, balling her fists at her sides. "What am I supposed to do?"

The pharmacist cleared his throat nervously. "Miss Hunter, you know this isn't my fault. I would gladly give it to you if I could."

"Eliza," Benjamin called and put his arm around her stiffened body. "Hey, maybe we can work this out. What's the damage?" he asked, and looked at the bill. "Whoa," he said. "I can see why you're upset." He looked at the pharmacist. "Ken, you gotta call the doctor on this one."

"I'll do that, but he may substitute a different medication. Is that what you want?" Ken asked. Benjamin knew the pharmacist had filled many prescriptions for Eliza and knew that finding the right medication for her condition seemed to be an ongoing struggle.

"He'll put me on that stuff before that made me

feel all cloudy," Eliza said. "I'd rather go without if I have to take that."

Benjamin's gut tightened at the idea of his sister going without any meds. Her lows had turned dangerous more than once. "Let me take a look at that bill again."

"You can't pay that. It's ridiculous," Eliza said.

Benjamin waved his hand. "Ken, how about you call the doctor? We'll come back in an hour."

"The doctor may not call me back, and I close at six tonight," Ken said. "I can stretch it to six fifteen, but my wife won't be happy."

"Okay. Just do your best. We'll be back before you close." Benjamin turned to his sister. "Let's go to the bar. I'll get you a burger and some onion rings. You look like you could use some comfort food."

"I haven't felt hungry lately," she said. "It's a shame you don't serve milk shakes."

"We have ice cream. I'm sure Jimmy can come up with something for you. Come on. You can tell me about the jewelry you've been making," he said, urging her out the door and down the street.

"You must really be desperate if you're asking to hear about my jewelry," she said. "I wasn't ready to jump off a cliff back there. I was just getting anxious. That's why I sent you a text."

"And that's why I'm here," he said.

"I thought you were supposed to be taking your fishing vacation at the lodge," she said.

"I am. Kinda," he said. "Jedediah's daughters are

giving the place a face-lift. I think they're going to try to bring in more paying guests."

"How do you feel about that?" she asked.

He shrugged. "They're trying to keep it running. It may bring a little business my way, too."

"Not that you're hurting since you own the only bar in town," she said as they arrived at the door to his business.

"I try to keep up with what customers want," he said and waved to Jimmy behind the bar. "Two orders of burgers and onion rings. If you can rustle up a milk shake for the lady, that would be great. I'll take water."

"You can have beer," Eliza said. "It won't tempt me. I've learned alcohol and these meds don't mix," she said.

"Glad to hear it, but I'll stick with water for now. So, tell me about your jewelry," he said.

"Tell me about the Jackson girls first. You were older and got to spend time at the lodge when I didn't. Plus, it seemed like they were only here during the summers. I always heard they were high society. Can't imagine them doing any physical labor."

Benjamin smiled, picturing Vivian with paint smeared on her face. "Looks like they're all painting machines right now. They're trying to get the lodge ready for wedding season."

Eliza's eyes widened. "Wedding season? Who would want to get married at a hunting and fishing lodge?"

"You'd be surprised. They've gotten the wiring

and plumbing redone on the cabins. Now they're painting the lodge," he said.

"Why don't they just pay someone to do it?"

Benjamin rubbed his fingers together. "Jedediah left the lodge, but not a lot of cash."

"Oh. I'm surprised they didn't just sell it," she said, smiling her thanks at the bartender when he delivered their meals.

"I think they considered it, but something changed their minds."

"Hmm," she said, munching on an onion ring. "I heard they always wore designer clothes and had perfect hair."

"I think their mother was a perfectionist. They seem pretty nice to me. A little nervous about making it all work, but nice."

"But not pretty," she said.

"I didn't say that."

"Oh."

"Tell me about your jewelry," he said.

Eliza gave him a knowing grin. "I wonder if my brother has a crush on one of them."

"Jewelry," he returned, determined not to bite. Eliza could turn into a real snoop if she wanted. He'd always kept his meager love life private from her, and he didn't want to start stirring up her interest now.

The arrival of her milk shake distracted her slightly, and he told her to hustle with consuming her meal so they could get back to the pharmacy.

A few minutes later, it only took one look at Ken's

face to see they were stuck with either no news or bad news. "I'm sorry," Ken said. "They didn't get back in touch with me. I'll get in touch with them tomorrow for you."

Benjamin could feel his sister fretting, although the only visible sign was the knotting and unknotting of her fingers.

"Can we get half the prescription?" Benjamin asked.

"Benjamin, no—" Eliza began.

"I can cover it. I haven't bought any Maseratis lately," he joked.

"Sure, you can take half," Ken said. "I'll ring it up for you and call the doctor again tomorrow."

After Benjamin paid for the prescription and they left the pharmacy, he walked her to her car. "You want me to come over tonight?"

She shook her head. "No. I'm okay. Burger, onion rings, milk shake and new drugs. I didn't sleep well last night, so I'm hoping tonight will be better." She must've spotted the concern on his face even though he thought he was so good at concealing it. She gave him a light punch. "Stop worrying. I'm going to a support group meeting tomorrow."

"Hey, that's great news. How far do you have to drive?" he asked.

"Just twenty-five miles. I can do that." She sighed, then gave him a big hug. "Thanks for being such a good brother."

Forty-five minutes later, Benjamin walked toward the dock with a beer in his hand. When he saw Vivian seated and leaning against a post, he stopped, wondering if he should turn around and go to his room. After his time with his sister, he felt edgy. At the moment, he wasn't full of easy comebacks or jokes.

"Hey, stranger," she called out.

She must have spotted him. Benjamin walked the dock and slid down to sit opposite her. "Sorry I didn't bring your wine. I thought this might be too late for you."

"No problem. I've got my own," she said, lifting her mostly full glass. "Problems?"

"Just putting out a fire before it gets out of control," he said, popped open his can and took a deep swallow.

"You want to talk about it?" she asked.

"Not really," he said. "How's Jet?"

"Back to comatose," she said. "He's favoring his paw. I can't say I blame him. I gave him some of the pain medication from the vet."

"That's good," he said.

Silence stretched between them.

"Listen, Vivian, I may not be the best company tonight. I've got some things on my mind," he said.

"But you don't want to talk about them," she said.

"No."

"Okay. I guess this also means you don't want to go swimming in the lake," she said, trying to get a smile out of him.

He met her gaze, and she saw a glint in his eye. "Are you offering to go first?"

Her breath hitched at the underlying challenge in his tone. "It's a little chilly tonight," she said. "Even you are wearing a jacket."

"Then why did you suggest it?" he asked.

"To help you get back a little sense of humor." She shook her head at herself. "I'm not helping," she muttered. "I should probably go." She started to leave, but he grabbed her hand.

"No need to rush off," he said. "Unless you mind just sitting for a while."

"I guess not," she said.

"Then come over here next to me. That'll put me in a better mood," he said and almost grinned.

She sank down beside him and rested her back against his arm. She closed her eyes and sighed, and she decided to stop worrying for just a moment. She pushed the dark anxiousness and what-ifs from her mind and listened to the water lap against the dock.

"That's a wonderful sound," she said in a low voice. "The water."

"You have to be quiet to hear it."

"Quiet in your mind," she added and turned slightly to look up at him. "You've been living close to the lake for ages. How often have you sat on a dock and listened to the water?"

"Not often enough. I've been busy growing the bar, and then I bought an auto repair shop. I invested in the bakery/ice-cream shop. Not sure how that last one happened."

"You've been busy building your empire," she said.

He chuckled. "I'm not sure I'd call it an empire,

but it has kept me busy. I always liked taking this break at the lodge. I was close enough for emergencies with people or issues, but I wasn't in the middle of everything. And now that I've talked the new boss into letting me stay longer..." He lowered his head and nuzzled her forehead.

Vivian relished the sensation. This was a practically perfect moment in an imperfect day. Lifting her head, she brushed her cheek against his, which was just a little rough from his slight beard.

Benjamin lowered his mouth to hers and kissed her sweetly, deeply. She savored the sensation of his warmth and strength.

The kiss seemed to go on and on, and Vivian grew warmer. She wanted to push her hands beneath his shirt to feel his bare skin, but she stopped herself. The temptation made her feel a little light-headed.

Benjamin pulled away for a short, breathless moment and held her gaze. The desire she saw rocketed through her. He lowered his mouth again, and this time he slid his hands underneath her shirt. His hands were warm, searching and clever. After releasing the clasp of her bra, her cupped one of her breasts and rubbed his thumb over her nipple.

Vivian couldn't resist the urge to press into his hand.

"Like that, huh? I do, too," he murmured against her mouth. He pulled her on top of him, positioning her so she could feel that he was aroused.

Vivian instinctively rubbed against him and he

groaned, squeezing her hips. Vivian strained toward him. She wanted more. She wanted him.

He pulled back slightly. "Viv, if we keep going like this, I'm not gonna want to stop," he said.

She bit her lip and tried to stick to reason, but she wanted him more than the warning bell clanging in her brain. "I don't want to stop, either," she said and ran her hands over his skin.

He hissed at her touch and pulled her back to his mouth. His kiss spoke of dark, raw need, and something inside her echoed the emotion right back at him. He stripped off her shirt and his, but kept her warm in his arms.

"Cold?" he asked.

Vivian shook her head, reveling in the sensation of her breasts against his chest. The night air was cool, but he was hot and making her hotter with each passing moment. He dropped his mouth to her breasts, and she arched into him.

She couldn't remember feeling wanted this much. She couldn't remember wanting this much. He unfastened her jeans and pushed them down, along with her panties. His hands were warm as he caressed her between her legs and she grew damp and restless.

Moving against him, she pulled his mouth to his and kissed him, drawing his tongue into her mouth. His groan of approval aroused her even more, and she reached down to undo his jeans. He was warm and hard, and she enjoyed touching him as intimately as he had touched her.

"Oh, Viv," he said. "I'm not going to be able to stand much of that."

"I want you to feel the way I do," she whispered.

"Lady, I'm already there," he told her and laid his jacket beneath her on the dock. Shucking his jeans, he pulled protection from his pocket.

A breeze flowed over her body, and for just a second she felt a chill. But he covered her with his warmth.

"How did you just happen to have a condom in your pocket?" she asked, smiling into his eyes.

"I told you. The way you make me feel, I always want to be ready. Now I'm going to make sure you're ready, too."

He kissed and caressed his way down her body and back up again until it was all she could do not to beg him to finish her. She felt as if she were in full sensual bloom and need. She might not be verbally begging, but her body sure was.

Touching him again intimately, she found him even harder with need. "Oh, Viv, I've got to have you." He put on the protection and plunged inside her.

His gaze locking with hers, he moved in a rhythm that took them both higher and higher. Sensation chased emotion, and Vivian felt herself burst into a powerful climax. Seconds later, Benjamin thrust deep inside her and stiffened, groaning in pleasure.

Still bracing himself on his forearms, he sank closer to her, kissing her throat. "How'd you get to be so good and bad at the same time?" he asked her.

"I didn't know I was," she said, trying to catch her breath. She wrapped her arms around his shoulders, holding him close, wanting to stay in his embrace as long as possible.

Benjamin rolled onto his back and pulled her on top of him. "You okay?" he asked in sexy, husky voice. "Wanna go again?"

"Oh, wow," she said, feeling a wicked thrill. "Yes, but I'm starting to feel that cool breeze."

"Can't have that," he said and dragged his jacket from beside them to cover her back.

Vivian snuggled against him, savoring the moment, because she knew it couldn't last forever.

"You're quiet," he said. "Regrets already?"

"None," she told him, meeting his gaze. "But I may be a little sex-drunk."

"I'll have to see if I can keep you that way," Benjamin said.

"That could be dangerous," she said.

"I'm willing to try it," he said and took her mouth.

Vivian felt a combination of thrill and fear. She needed to keep the reins on her heart. She'd learned that when she didn't, things could go badly.

Chapter Eight

Vivian slept so hard she drooled on her pillow and awakened an hour past the time she usually rose. After glancing at her clock, she scrambled out of bed and took a quick shower and dressed. She tried not to think about making love with Benjamin last night, but her body reminded her with subtle aches and awareness. She'd forgotten sex could be a workout, or maybe it never had been for her before.

Grabbing an energy bar and a cup of coffee, she gave a quick greeting to Grayson and checked on Jet. The dog seemed to be resting well. Climbing the stairs, she waved at Jilly and mouthed, "Good morning," since Jilly was wearing her earphones.

"Hello. This is looking great," she said to Temple,

pausing on her way to the room she hoped to finish painting today.

"Thanks," Temple said. "Where have you been?"

"I overslept. I guess some of the stress just caught up with me," she said, even though she knew Benjamin was the reason she'd slept so well.

"You're not sick, are you?" Temple asked, walking toward her, studying her more closely.

"No. I'm fine," Vivian said, feeling self-conscious. Even though she knew Temple couldn't see what Vivian had done on the dock last night, she still felt uncomfortable under her scrutiny. "That extra hour of sleep did wonders. I'll head on to my assigned room since I'm a bit behind schedule."

"Wait a minute." Temple frowned. "What's wrong with your neck? It looks like you have a bruise," she said, lifting her finger. "If you were a teenager, I'd suspect a hickey. Have you been having a little too much fun with Benjamin?"

Vivian felt a rush of heat to her face and prayed it didn't show. "Oh, of course not. It's not as if I have gobs of extra time." She rubbed at her neck. "I must have scratched it when I was in the woods looking for Jet yesterday. I was so frantic to find him, I must not have noticed."

"It doesn't look like a scratch," Temple mused.

"Well, it must have happened yesterday. I can't think of anything else. It's not bothering me, so I imagine it will go away soon. I really should get on with painting if we're going to meet our goal. I'll see you at lunch. Okay?"

Temple nodded. "Okay. Don't work too hard. We don't need you getting sick."

"I'm fine. Thanks, though," Vivian said over her shoulder as she headed down the hallway. As soon as she entered the bedroom she was painting, she darted into the bathroom to look in the mirror. Sure enough, she saw a bruise on the side of her neck. Swearing, she released her hair from its ponytail in order to cover the telltale mark. She would have to give Benjamin instructions to be more careful next time. She caught herself at the thought and swore again. Not that there would be a next time.

Benjamin caught a few fish that morning, but they were either too small or they were carp. Nothing worth eating. His mind was mostly on Vivian. He hadn't expected her to be such a daring lover, but she'd been hot enough to fry him inside and out, and now he wanted more. Not just sex. He wanted more time with her, period.

After he cleaned up, he meandered down the hallway to the room she was painting. With her backside facing him, he couldn't help thinking about how he'd squeezed her last night. He came up behind her and put his hands on her hips.

"Aren't you ready for some lunch?"

Vivian squealed, whirling so quickly to face him that he had to dodge her paintbrush. "Whoa," he said, steadying her hand.

"You startled me. What are you doing, sneaking up behind me like that?" she demanded.

"I wasn't sneaking. You just didn't hear me," he said. "What's got your panties in a twist?"

"I think Temple may suspect you and I—" she hesitated "—got together last night. I don't want anyone to know. I don't want to be teased. I don't want the speculation."

"Why would she suspect?" he asked.

"Because you gave me a hickey!" she said in the most outraged whisper he'd ever heard. She lifted her hair to reveal the mark.

"Oops. I don't remember..." He shrugged. "Gotta tell you, I pretty much wanted to consume you. I guess I shouldn't be surprised."

Color rose to her cheeks. "Well, you need to be more careful when we—" She cleared her throat. "If we," she corrected herself.

"I'll do my best, but you're hell on my control. I'm wondering if I might affect you the same way," he said and pulled back his collar so that she could see the mark she'd left on his neck.

Her eyes widened in shock, and she covered her mouth. "Oh, my, no." She shook her head. "Are you sure I did that? I mean, I've never—not that I can remember, anyway." She closed her eyes, clearly mortified. "I apologize."

"Don't," he said and pulled her into his arms. "If I'm the first guy you gave a hickey, then I'm honored. You can even do it again if the mood strikes," he said and chuckled as he brushed his mouth over her forehead.

She glanced up at him. "It's not funny. I'd like to

keep our relationship secret. I don't want to draw attention."

"I'm not really big on secrets. I've had to deal with a few in my lifetime, and they can turn into a big burden," he said, thinking of his sister and his parents' relationship. "But I get that you want to be discreet. I'll try not to attack you when you're around other people."

That afternoon while Vivian painted and tried not to think about Benjamin, her cell phone rang with an unfamiliar number on the caller ID. She considered not answering because her work calls were filtered through the office, but shrugged and picked up. "Vivian Jackson," she said, surveying her painting job.

"Hello, Vivian, this is Corinne Whitman Jergenson. Your friend Sela Warren mentioned you are opening a lake house as an intimate wedding venue. My daughter is getting married. Third marriage," she murmured in a low voice. "We'd like to do this soon. We've been visiting my mother in Ashville, and I wondered if Olive and I could pop by your lakeside villa for a peek."

Vivian nearly dropped her phone. She'd always thought Sela Warren looked down on her as if Vivian weren't quite good enough, despite the fact that the two of them were active in several charities in Atlanta. Perhaps she did look down on her, if she'd sent *the* Corinne Whitman Jergenson, whose father owned a quarter of the state of Georgia.

"I'm so flattered. I don't know what to say. We are nowhere ready to entertain guests. In fact, I'm pa—I'm supervising refurbishment even at this moment."

"No problem. Olive and I have vivid imaginations. We can picture the possibilities."

Vivian clenched her jaw and took a deep breath. "Well, I fear Sela may have embellished. You know what a positive person she is. Honeymoon Mountain Lake is more of a hunting and fishing lodge with cabins."

The deep sound of silence stretched.

Vivian counted to ten, then decided to rescue both herself and *the* Corinne from continuing discomfort. "I really appreciate your interest, but—"

"We'd still like to visit," Corinne said. "Olive's husband-to-be is a professional bass fisherman. And since it's her third marriage... We'll arrive in two hours. See you soon."

"But. But. But." Vivian realized she was speaking to air. "Oh, crap," she said and darted from the room.

"Corinne Whitman Jergenson is coming," she yelled. "We need to straighten up, clean up, make everything perfect," she said, trying to keep her panic from her voice.

Temple peeked her head outside a room down the hall. "Who is Corinne Whitman Jergenson?" she asked.

"She's big. Very big. High society in Atlanta. If we impress her, she will say wonderful things about us."

"So, why is she coming here?" Temple asked.

"It's her daughter's third wedding. I guess they're hedging their bets," Vivian said. "Start cleaning and straightening, please."

Vivian continued down the hall and found Jillian happily painting. Her sister was wearing earphones and wiggling her butt as she painted. Vivian knew yelling would do no good, so she tapped Jilly on the shoulder.

Her sister jumped, splattering paint everywhere.

Vivian swallowed several swearwords.

Jillian pulled out her earphones. "What? Why did you startle me?"

"How do I not startle you when you're wearing earphones?"

Jillian frowned. "Well." She scowled. "I don't know. What do you want?"

"We have a big-time potential client coming, so we need to clean up as quickly as we can."

"Now?" Jillian asked.

"Five minutes ago."

"Who could be that important?"

"She's a very influential woman from Atlanta. If she praises us, we'll be getting bookings with no problems. Her approval is great advertising."

"And if she doesn't like the lodge?" Jillian asked.

Vivian made a face. "Let's not think about that."

She crammed as much as she could into closets and fluffed the pillows on the sofa and chairs on the porch. As she headed to the bar with a dust rag, a knock sounded at the front door.

Wincing, she stuffed the rag in a cabinet and

raced to the door. Just as she opened the door, she realized her hair was in a ponytail and she might still have paint on her face. *Alrighty.*

Vivian flung open the door and gave her best smile. "Hello, and welcome to Honeymoon Lodge. I wish we could have been better prepared for your visit. Please come in and bear in mind that we're making improvements."

Corrine Whitman Jergenson smiled. Her lips moved, but the rest of her face did not. Neither did her hair. Olive wore so much eye makeup and contouring cream.

Olive smiled, however, and the rest of her face moved, so Vivian felt a smidge of relief.

"This looks so charming and rustic. I just know Bubba would approve of it," Olive said. "He loves hunting and fishing, and I know he loves me for me."

"Yes, dear," Corinne said. "Let's take a look around first. I must ask," she said to Vivian, "where would you hold the ceremony?"

"We have limited space for large gatherings. Some people use the foyer for their weddings. The stairway offers a grand entrance and can be decorated as you wish."

"It's a bit small," Corinne said.

Vivian's stomach knotted. "Yes. I'm not sure what size group you want to accommodate."

"We're not, either," Corinne muttered.

"We also offer two outside venues," Vivian said and led them through the screened-in porch to view the outdoor dock. "If you want a larger group, we can accommodate a wedding by the lake."

"Oh, that's beautiful," Olive said. "Bubba would love it."

"What if it rains?" Corinne countered.

"Tents can be rented," Vivian said.

"But the mud," Corinne said with a frown.

"There is one other option in our bar area," Vivian said, walking back to the lodge. "We can remove seating. It would be cozy. After the ceremony, we could open the bar and other areas to accommodate the guests."

Corinne glanced around the area. "It's a bit dark, but not bad. With a little extra lighting, it could work."

"I like the outside better," Olive said.

"Outside venues get too expensive with the need for tents and temperature control, especially since we'd be at the mercy of the weather," Corinne said. "I can see possibilities here. How many bedrooms are available?"

"We have fifteen rooms in the lodge and seven cabins. I must remind you that our accommodations are more rustic than luxury."

"Does that mean our guests will use outhouses?"

"Oh, no," Vivian said. "Our cabins are furnished with comfortable linens, heat and air-conditioning, bathrooms, and a microwave and minifridge."

Corinne waved her hand. "That's more than many luxury resorts offer. Plus, you have an amazing view." She paused. "And it's only one weekend."

Vivian somehow felt as if she'd been patted and slapped at the same time, but forced a smile. "Well, thank you so much for stopping by."

The back door flung open and Jet ambled into the room with Benjamin behind him, carting a cooler. Jet dumped a dead fish at Vivian's feet.

Benjamin glanced from Vivian to the visitors and shook his head. "Jet got out again. He grabbed one of my fish. I guess he was determined to bring it to you."

Despite the disdainful glare of Corinne, Vivian knew what she had to do. Poor Jet had been depressed for so long. She bent down and petted him. "Sweet boy. You're such a good boy. Jet was my father's dog," she began.

Olive wrinkled her nose. "That smell. Is it the fish?"

Unfortunately not. The *smell* was Jet. Before Vivian could say or do anything, she caught sight of Millicent at the bottom of the stairs, wearing a house robe. "Oh, dear," she said. "Do we have visitors? This is my first day I can take on the stairs by myself."

"Good for you," Vivian said. "I'm so pleased for you." She turned to Corinne. "Mrs. Jergenson, I know you can appreciate overcoming a disabling injury. Everyone is familiar with your charity work."

Corinne lifted her chin with an expression of pride. "Yes, of course I understand. I've volunteered many hours of my time, and my husband has even donated a wing to the hospital." She walked to Millicent and offered her hand. "Congratulations on your improvement. I'm sure you'll be back to your old self in no time." She then turned to her daughter. "Olive, we should go. Miss Jackson, thank you for your hospitality. We'll contact you if we need further information."

"Thank you for stopping by," Vivian said, and the door closed behind Corinne and her daughter.

Her sisters appeared suddenly as if they'd been hiding in the woodwork. "How do you think it went?" Temple asked.

Vivian glanced down at Jet and the dead fish at her feet and sighed. "I don't know. It seemed like Corinne wanted to downsize the wedding this time."

"Well, it is Olive's third time down the aisle, isn't it?" Temple asked.

"Still," Vivian said, her stomach sinking. "I hope I didn't blow it."

"You didn't blow it," Benjamin said with a shrug. "I thought you handled the dead fish very well."

His encouragement eased some of her anxiety. At the same time, Vivian felt uncomfortable with the idea of counting on Benjamin. Booking this wedding was on her shoulders, not his. "Thanks. Now, what to do about Jet's odor?"

"I'll take care of it," Jillian said. "I've been thinking about this, and now is the time. I'm going to give Jet a bath. Inside."

Vivian winced. "Are you sure that's a good idea? We don't want him tearing up a bathroom."

"It will be fine," she said. "I'm going to give Jet

a spa experience. You know, I once worked at a spa," she said.

"I didn't know that, but I'm not really surprised because you seem to have become a jack-of-all-trades," Vivian said. "Do you want some help?"

"Nope," Jillian said. "I figure three or four hamburgers should distract him enough to get the job done. I'll go fix them right now."

Vivian, Temple and Benjamin watched as Jillian headed to the kitchen, her shoulders squared with determination.

"She's brave," Vivian said.

"Yes, she is. I'll get back to painting," Temple said and walked away.

"I'd better help her," Vivian said.

"Meet me on the dock later?" Benjamin asked.

Vivian shook her head. She clearly needed to get control of herself. "Not tonight."

Ignoring the terrible longing to escape with Benjamin, she joined Jilly in the kitchen, where her sister was putting frozen burgers in the microwave. "I can do this by myself," Jilly said. "And the great thing about Jet is that he won't care that I microwaved the burgers. Why don't you spend some time with Benjamin? You could use it."

"What do you mean, I could use it?" Vivian asked.

Jilly shrugged. "You just seem a little less tense after you've been with Benjamin. Otherwise, you're kinda…" Jilly broke off as she peeked at the progress of the burgers.

"I'm kinda what?" Vivian said.

"I don't know. Tense, a little cranky," Jilly said and slid a sideways glance at her. "Don't get mad at me."

"I'm not mad," Vivian said. "I guess I just didn't realize it was showing that much."

"Well, we're together 24/7, so the real you is going to leak out sometimes."

"Nice to know the real me is so disagreeable," Vivian muttered.

Jilly shook her head as the microwave dinged. "You're not disagreeable all the time. But you have to admit you're worried. You feel responsible for everything, more than you should."

Vivian sighed.

"My offer for morning yoga is still open," Jilly said.

"I have a hard time concentrating during yoga. My mind wanders," Vivian said.

"See Benjamin, then. He's the reason why your mind is wandering," Jilly said. "Time for Jet's bath."

Vivian didn't call Benjamin, but she kept thinking about him. Jilly set the spa mood in the bathroom with soothing Zen music and dimmed lights for the dog. Despite Jilly's best efforts, when they corralled Jet into the bathroom and hoisted him into the tub, he howled and whined as if they were killing him.

Jilly and Vivian kept encouraging him and giving him bites of burger as they scrubbed away his dirt and stink. After a few minutes, he became distracted by the bites of burger and let Jilly have her way with him.

By the end of the ordeal, he still smelled like a wet dog, but a cleaner wet dog. Drenched and exhausted, Vivian looked at Jilly. "There's got to be an easier way. Next time we'll pay the vet to do it."

Jilly shook her head. "Jet is so difficult that I'm not sure even the vet would be willing to do it," she said. "But we can tell everyone in this house not to let him outside, and maybe that will help."

"And a little powder," Vivian said. "Remember how Dad said a little powder could make everything better?"

Jilly chuckled. "We can hope. I'm turning in early tonight. What about you?"

Vivian nodded and thought again of Benjamin. She reined in her unwelcome longing for him. "Me, too."

Chapter Nine

"Pizza delivery," Benjamin called as he knocked on the door of his sister's townhome.

Seconds passed and the door flung open. Eliza laughed up at him. "What a nice surprise. Why are you here? I've been okay lately."

"Surprise pizza is not dependent on your health. In fact, we all need pizza."

"Well, I'll take it," she said, grabbing the box from him. "But what did I do to deserve this visit?"

"Nothing," Benjamin said with a shrug. "I just wanted to visit my sister. How's everything going?" he asked, glancing at the kitchen table, where she had been creating jewelry.

"Good," she said. "I'm doing shows the next few weeks. But what's going on with you?" she asked.

"Nothing. Just taking some time off and fishing," he said.

"Hmm. Why don't I believe you?"

"I don't know," he said. "Why don't you?"

"I think you're under the spell of one of those Jackson girls," she said.

"I'm not under the spell of anyone or anything," he said, even though he felt Vivian's presence in his brain. "I keep a clear head. I have to."

His sister frowned. "Now I feel guilty because I know you have to keep a clear head because of me."

"Don't feel guilty. I have to keep a clear head for everything in my life. It's not a bad thing," he said. "Now, let's eat some pizza and you show me your new jewelry."

"You're dodging me," Eliza said. "But I'm hungry."

While they gobbled down the pizza, Eliza showed him the bracelets, necklaces and earrings she'd created with multicolored stones and hammered metal. Her enthusiasm and intensity about her art had always warmed his heart. Even when she was a little girl, Eliza had always loved art. One of the first signs that she was on a downward turn was a lack of interest in art.

At the moment, though, she seemed to be doing well.

"You sleeping?" he asked.

"Some," she said. "Are you diagnosing me? Because I don't want it right now."

"Just asking," he said with a shrug, but he wondered.

"Don't worry. I have a lot to get done for these shows, but I'm sleeping. Really."

"Good," he said, although he still worried.

"Good," she said. "I think one of those Jackson girls is on your mind. Don't lie to me. Is she trying to rope you into marriage?"

He laughed. "That couldn't be further from the truth." He hesitated a half beat. "She wants to hide our relationship."

"Whoa." She stared at him in surprise. "That's new. Don't most of your girls want you to marry them?"

He shot her a sideways glance.

"Well, maybe except for that one from college who didn't like the idea of settling down in a small town." She shrugged. "I hope it works out how you want it to. I doubt I'll ever marry. I'm still learning how to deal with all my ups and downs. It's hard enough on my brother and me."

"Don't say that," he said. "You've got a lot going for you. I just wish you felt like you could be a little more open with people."

"So they'll think I'm sick? No, thank you. I'm not ready for that. I don't want to be pitied."

Benjamin sighed. "Pity and sympathy and empathy are different. I know for a fact that you're not the only person who struggles."

"How do you know that?" she challenged him.

"I own a bar," he said. "You wouldn't believe all the stories I've heard."

"And just like a therapist or a priest, you never tell," she said.

"I've never liked to gossip," he said and knew the reason. People had gossiped about his father for years. As a trucker, his father had spent most of his time away from home. There'd been talk that he had cheated on his mother. Benjamin didn't like the thought of it but knew it was a possibility. Since his father had died in his teens, there were a lot of unanswered questions. Not the kind of questions he would have wanted to ask his mother, especially given her fragile health.

"Saint Benjamin," she teased.

"You know that's not true. If I were a saint, I wouldn't take the last piece of pizza," he said as he snatched the slice and smiled before he took a big bite.

Benjamin almost didn't go back to the lake, but something drew him. It was a cloudy night, but he spotted Vivian perched on the end of the dock, swinging her legs like a little girl. He could almost swear, however, that he saw the weight of the world on those slim but deceptively strong shoulders. Something about the sight of her made his gut tighten. His response to her still caught him off guard.

As he walked toward her, she turned to look at him. "Hi," she said in a soft voice.

"Hi to you," he said, but didn't sit down to join her on the dock.

"I should apologize for acting so cranky with you," she said.

He swallowed a chuckle. "Does that mean you *are* apologizing? Or just that you think should?"

"I apologize. I freaked and took it out on you. I'm sorry," she said.

"Apology accepted," he said and sat down beside her. "You're still worried," he added, glancing at the lake, then back at her.

She nodded. "I haven't heard from Corinne Whitman Jergenson." She paused. "But I did hear from my mother."

"Not a sparkling experience?" he asked.

She gave a wry chuckle. "Not," she said. "I can usually dodge her questions by steering the conversation back to her and my stepfather. But it didn't work this time. I think she senses that both Temple and I have been avoiding her. Neither of us wanted to tell her that we were at Honeymoon Mountain, trying to repair it and make it profitable."

"It's not like you've formed a crime ring. What's so wrong with the three of you pulling together and making this a successful joint effort?"

"Just everything. My mother has very specific ideas and plans for the people in her life. The best way to describe it is, her life is an engine and we are parts of that engine and must play our roles. Trust me, none of her plans include having her daughters bring a hunting lodge back to life."

"Is that why none of you live near her?" he asked.

"That's one reason," she said and shook her head. "She's still not over the fact that I divorced my husband. She told me I should look the other way and give it another try after he got another woman pregnant."

"You're joking," he said.

"No. She said she didn't know if she would survive the scandal among her friends." She sighed. "It seems like she changed after she left my father and got remarried. Everything was about appearances. I went to a private girls' school. I had a lisp, so the other kids made fun of me. My mother was determined that I make friends with the right people, so I saw a speech therapist. It took a while, but I finally lost the lisp. She was so thrilled when it was gone." Vivian glanced down, then up again. "Of course, I was glad, too, and relieved. I was very fortunate that she had the determination and resources to help me."

Silence stretched between them. "But?" he prompted.

She stretched her neck from side to side to relieve tension. "It's going to sound weird, but I remember visiting my father after I'd finally lost the lisp. He said, 'Your little girl voice is gone.' I nodded. He said, 'I'll miss that, but good job. Good for you.'" She bit her lip. "They were such opposites. She was all about appearances. He couldn't give a rip what people thought."

"And you've got the best of both," he said.

Vivian laughed. "They were both extreme, so I'm

not sure what is the best of both. My biggest fear is that my mom will show up here."

"Why?" he asked. "It's not like she has supernatural evil powers."

Vivian winced. "Sometimes it seems like she does. She can make you feel like the worst thing in the world. Or, on very, very rare occasions, she can make you feel like the best."

He shrugged. "If you let her."

"What do you mean?"

"It's all about power. If you don't give her the power, then she doesn't have it. She can't tell you if you're the worst or the best if you don't let her. I've had coaches who tried to manipulate me in good ways and bad ways. You have to choose who you let influence you."

"You sound so smart and sage," she said.

He laughed. "Sports are about power."

"Sometimes it's still hard for me to believe you left it behind," she said.

"I had something more important to do," he said.

"Maybe you should teach me more about sports," she said seductively.

"I can do that," he said and leaned toward her. She lifted her head toward him.

He took her mouth with his.

At the same time, there was a commotion behind them on the dock.

Vivian drew back. "Oh, my."

Benjamin heard a scream and a splash and instinctively rose. "What—"

"It's Temple. She fell into the lake. She doesn't swim that well," Vivian said, running down the dock. "Temple!" she yelled.

Benjamin raced toward the splash and jumped into the lake. He grabbed Temple and dragged her to shore.

"What were you doing?" Vivian yelled to her sister.

"What were you doing?" Temple yelled in return.

"I didn't dive into the lake at night!" Vivian said.

"I wasn't making out on the dock," Temple countered.

"A vapor was involved, but I'm not in charge of this discussion," Benjamin said.

"You're smoking?" Vivian exclaimed. "What in the world are you thinking? You know better than that. I can't believe you, of all people, are smoking."

"Mom called and grilled me today," Temple said.

"Oh," Vivian said. "I understand." She sighed and turned to Benjamin winced. "I'm sorry you got wet. We can talk another time? Thank you. Temple and I need to go in now."

"By all means," he said, because he truly didn't want to get involved in a sister battle.

"You're shivering," Vivian said to Temple. "We need to get you back to the lodge." She urged her sister up the path to the main building. "I'm sorry Mom called you today. She called me, too. I have been putting her off, but I wasn't as successful today."

"Neither was I," Temple said, her teeth chattering. "My biggest fear is that she'll show up here unannounced."

"I've been worried about the same thing," Vivian confessed, guiding her sister down the hallway. "I was hoping her social activities would keep her too busy."

"If she's calling both you and me, she's clearly not busy enough. I just hope she won't try to call Jilly. Jilly is so fragile after being rejected by Mom."

Vivian grabbed a towel as they trudged into Temple's room. "The great thing about Jilly is that she has changed her contact numbers so many times."

"Yes, but Mom can be a pain when it comes to finding people."

Vivian scrubbed her sister with a towel. "I think you need to get into a hot shower."

"I think you're right," Temple said and went to the bathroom.

Vivian heard her sister turn on the spray. Seconds later, Temple called out, "I haven't forgotten that you were making out with Benjamin."

"I was hoping you had," Vivian whispered under her breath. "Get warm," she called.

A few moments later, Temple emerged wearing a towel on her head and a robe. She shot Vivian a questioning brow. "So, what's up with Benjamin?"

"It's supposed to be a secret," Vivian confessed.

"So, this isn't the first time you had a rendezvous on the dock?" Temple asked.

Vivian frowned. "I really don't like discussing this."

"As I don't like discussing my e-cigarette."

Vivian took a deep breath. "Okay. We're kinda involved."

"How involved?"

"Deep, but not forever," Vivian said.

"How do you know it's not forever?" Temple asked.

"Because I'm too busy for forever. I have to make things happen for the lodge," Vivian said.

"Hmm. I'm not sure it will work that way," Temple said.

"Should we discuss your e-cig?" Vivian asked.

"No. I smoked a little when I was in college. You know I finished my degree in three years. I was tempted when I was getting my advanced degrees, but I resisted. It's just since Dad died," Temple said.

"Is this my fault? I shouldn't have pressured you into helping with the lodge," Vivian said.

"No. I want to do this. I just have to manage my partnership and…"

"Do you need to go back to Charlotte? Go back. Go—"

"And there's Mom," Temple interrupted.

"Oh. Sorry," Vivian said.

Temple took a deep breath. "It's okay. Better now that we both know she's after us. Whatever we do, we need to protect Jilly from her."

"Truth," Vivian said and lifted her hand.

Temple lifted hers and pressed it against Vivian's. "Maybe it would be better if we didn't keep so many secrets from each other. Yes?"

"Yes," Vivian said and pulled her sister against her in a hug.

* * *

The following morning, Vivian and her sisters worked nonstop. Vivian still hadn't heard from Corinne Whitman Jergenson and refused to concentrate on that. If that deal didn't work out, another one would.

By the end of the day, she and her sisters ate cheeseburgers prepared by Jilly.

"Best burger in the world," Vivian said.

"Same," Temple said.

"You're just starving," Jilly said with a laugh.

"No, really," Vivian said. "Grilled onions and cheese."

"Mustard and steak sauce," Temple added.

Jilly laughed again. "Well, I'm glad you enjoyed them. By the way, have either of you heard from Mother?"

Vivian nearly choked. "Mother?"

"Yes," she said as she dipped her burger into a combined sauce of mustard and steak sauce. "I received a strange email. I've changed phones several times, so she can't reach me that way. I was surprised to hear from her because she doesn't contact me very often."

"What kind of email?" Temple asked, wiping her mouth. "There's a lot of spam out there."

"This looked legit," Jilly said. "She mentioned both of you. And Honeymoon Mountain."

Vivian swore under her breath. "Delete it. Please."

Vivian felt Jilly searching both her face and Temple's. "Why?"

"She doesn't like it that we're trying to make Honeymoon Mountain work," Vivian said. "Mom has talents and skills, but she can also be a negative influence. We don't need that right now."

"Hmm," Jilly said. "Maybe she needs yoga."

"Yeah," Temple said. "Good luck with that. Yoga meets the devil." She shook her head. "I didn't just say that."

"Of course you didn't," Vivian said, but she knew Jilly was watching and unfortunately hoping for a happily-ever-after with their mother. Vivian was determined to protect her little sister.

An hour later, Vivian holed herself in her room, working on the webpage for the resort. Although she was tired, she was determined to make headway. A knock sounded at her door. Vivian assumed it was one of her sisters. "Come on in," she called.

"Hello," a wonderfully familiar male voice said.

A delicious shiver raced down her spine, and she spun around to look at Benjamin. "What are you doing here?"

"I'm taking you away. You need to escape."

Chapter Ten

"Escape?" Vivian echoed, feeling a flash of excitement. "What do you have in mind?"

"Just trust me," he said. "Grab a cap and sunglasses."

"It's too dark for sunglasses," she said.

"They're only for emergency purposes," he said. "When you need to pretend you're a movie star in disguise."

She couldn't help giggling. "Movie star? Oh, this sounds fun."

"Are you in?" he asked.

"Yes," she said. "Let me grab my cap and sunglasses."

A moment later, she allowed him to lead her out the door, down the road of perdition. Sitting in his

SUV, she turned to him. "Are we going to a strip club?"

Benjamin stared at her in shock. "What the—" He shook his head. "No. This is mostly good, clean fun."

"Well, darn," she said.

He shot her a quick glance. "Are you serious?"

She laughed. "No. I'm giddy over the adventure. I've been so focused."

"Time to change your focus," he said and turned up the radio.

"I feel a little guilty," she said. "My sisters could use a change of focus, too."

"Tomorrow or the next day," he said. "Tonight is for you."

She laughed again. "I can't wait to see my escape."

He reached over and placed his hand over hers. "I think you'll like it."

Twenty minutes later, he drove into a small town.

"Where are we?" she asked.

"Crackerville," he said. "They hold a multicultural festival every year. Latin, Native American, Scottish, everything you can imagine. Put on your cap and you'll fit right in."

Vivian donned her cap and stepped out of his SUV to the competing sounds of Latin music and bagpipes. "What a combination," she said.

He chuckled and took her hand. "Embrace your escape," he said and led her into the crowd.

Latin dancers were teaching people their movements. "Go for it," he said and pushed her into the crowd.

Vivian glanced back at him, then did her best to follow the dances. She laughed throughout the routine. "Oh, pooh," she said as she stumbled repeatedly, but she made it through. She turned around to find Benjamin smiling as he watched her.

She ran toward him. "Happy now that I made a fool of myself?"

"You were no fool," he said. "You had great rhythm."

"You flatter me," she said and put her arm around his waist. "Where to next?"

"Let's eat something really bad," he suggested.

"That sounds good to me," she said.

After a round of shared brats and a funnel cake, Vivian grabbed her stomach. "I'm so full I can barely walk," she said, then saw a row of arts and crafts vendors. "Oh, wait. Let's go look at the crafts."

"Are you sure you don't want to sit down?" Benjamin asked.

She shook her head. "I need to walk off this full feeling. Might as well shop," she said with a smile.

"If you say so," he said, and they walked toward the vendors.

He watched her slide her fingers over scarves, and she even purchased one and asked for the artist's card. Next she admired pottery but didn't make a purchase. Then she arrived at a row of jewelers. At that moment, he felt an indescribable itch, as if this might not be the best idea. He glanced down the row, saw his sister showing her wares and decided they needed to leave. Immediately.

"Hey, does your stomach feel better? We should probably head back," he said, pulling down his cap and adjusting his sunglasses.

"What do you mean? We're just getting to the good stuff," she said and moved to the next vendor.

Benjamin wasn't sure if he should abandon her for a few moments or stick it out. He just didn't want Vivian and his sister to meet. He didn't welcome the questions that would follow from either of them.

Vivian viewed the jewelry from the first two vendors, then moved to his sister's stall. "Oh, wow," she said. "This is stunning, and you have so much to offer. I love the blue topaz, and the jade is gorgeous."

"Thank you," his sister said. "I've been busy. I'm always trying new ways—" She looked at Benjamin and broke off. "Hey, there," she said. "Are you going to introduce me?"

Benjamin sighed. He was caught. "Eliza, this is Vivian," he said. "Eliza is my sister," he added.

Vivian's eyes rounded. "Oh," she said. "I'm so pleased to meet you."

"Same for me," Eliza said. "I thought you would be more prissy."

Benjamin rolled his eyes. Thank goodness his expression was hidden by his sunglasses.

Vivian opened her mouth, then shut it, as if she was searching for a response. "Well, I've spent a lot of time painting the lodge," she managed.

"Oh, it wasn't a criticism," Eliza said. "You're just so naturally pretty. And nice."

Vivian glanced at Benjamin. "I don't know what you've heard about me, but I do try to be kind. Mean is ugly every language."

Eliza laughed. "So true. I think you and I would get along just fine."

"I love your work, but I'm finding it hard to choose," Vivian said, clearly changing the subject.

"Blue topaz necklace," Eliza said. "It will match your eyes. It's on me."

"Oh, no, you're too generous," Vivian said, pulling money from her pocket. "May I have your card?"

"Sure," Eliza said. She reluctantly accepted Vivian's money, then reached up to press her lips against Benjamin's cheek. "She's nicer than I expected."

"Yeah, great," Benjamin said and gently pulled Vivian away from his sister's jewelry stall.

"She's darling," Vivian said. "A little outspoken," she added.

"That's putting it mildly," he muttered.

"What do you mean?" she asked. "You almost act as if you didn't want her to meet me."

"How quickly we forget," he said. "You didn't want to out me to your sisters."

"Well, that's different. I have to lead. They need to believe that I'm level and unaffected by my hormones."

"So I make you hormonal?" he asked.

She playfully slapped at him. "Times ten."

"But I don't involve your intellect?" he said.

"You involve everything. That's why you're so much trouble," she said and reached up to kiss him.

Benjamin drove back to the lodge and stopped just before the door in case Vivian was trying to go incognito. She turned to him. "This was wonderful. You have no idea how much I needed it." She lifted her head toward him, and his mouth immediately took hers.

Their kiss quickly turned passionate. Vivian squeezed his shoulders. He trailed his hands toward her breasts.

The windows fogged.

Vivian dropped her head to his chest. "I know this sounds strange, but I want us to go a little slower."

Although he was aroused, he ground his teeth to settle down. "Good idea."

"But hard," she said.

"You have no idea," he said.

She stroked his jaw, and that touch made him feel tender and loved. "I'm sorry."

"It's okay," he said. "I'll take a cold shower."

"I will, too," she said and left his SUV.

Somehow, the fact that she would also be suffering gave him a little comfort.

Vivian didn't sleep well that night. Her bladder and hormones seemed to bother her. She couldn't get comfortable. Was she getting ready to start her period? It occurred to her when she rose the next morning that she might have rested much better if she and Benjamin had slept together. Such a forbidden thought, but heaven help her, she felt grumpy.

Pushing through her mood, she took a shower and pulled her hair back in a ponytail. She grabbed her laptop, walked to the kitchen, turned on the coffeemaker and strode to the porch, where Jilly was doing yoga.

"Namaste," Vivian said in a low voice.

Jilly struck a difficult pose. "Yeah," she said in a non-namaste voice.

"Are you okay?" Vivian asked.

Jillian took a deep breath. "I haven't actually spoken to Mother, but I still feel freaked out."

"Welcome to my world," Vivian said.

Jillian made a face. "I don't want to feel that way, so I think we should have a party."

"Excuse me?" Vivian said.

Jillian settled into a cross-legged pose. "I think we should have a party. Invite vendors we may need and include the community."

"It sounds like a lot of work," Vivian said.

"It sounds like a lot of money," Temple said as she walked into the screened-in porch. She shoved her hair out of her eyes and sighed as she sat down in a chair.

"It doesn't have to be a lot of work or money," Jillian said. "We could keep it easy with cakes and lemonade by Duane and Darcy. We could also limit the time, make it short and sweet. It would be good for our PR. You haven't heard back from the uptight Atlanta socialite, have you?"

"Not yet," Vivian said, and she was secretly losing hope.

"So, why not?" Jillian asked.

Temple sighed. "I can think of a million reasons why not, but maybe we should do it. Being static won't move us forward."

"Okay, let's do it," Vivian said. "I'll start compiling a guest list."

"And what's the news about you and Benjamin?" Jillian asked.

"I don't really want to talk about it," she said. "But he's pretty great." She lifted her hand. "Don't ask more."

"Chicken," Temple said.

"I could say something," Vivian said, thinking about Temple's vaping issue.

"Nothing, nothing, nothing," Temple said.

"What don't I know?" Jillian asked.

"Nothing, nothing, nothing," Temple repeated.

"Sounds like a lie to me," Jillian said.

"Namaste," Vivian said. "Trust me."

Jillian smiled. "Okay, namaste."

That afternoon, Vivian began to put together a list. The more she thought about it, the more she agreed that a party was a good idea. They'd done a lot of rehab on the lodge and the cabins. After all this work, they needed to round up the community in hopes of getting support. They would need plumbers, electricians for continuing maintenance and bed-and-breakfasts for support. There may be times when they will have an overflow of guests. This will be a short-notice invite.

Vivian talked with Grayson. "We need to make a signature drink for this party," she said.

"Rye whiskey and bourbon," he suggested.

She shook her head. "No. It needs to appeal to both women and men. We need two drinks so that there are options. Suggestions?" she asked.

"Old-fashioned Honeymoon Mountain," he said.

"Do I need to know what's in it?" she asked.

"Not really," he said. "Rye whiskey, Bourbon and a few other things."

"Okay, option two?" she said.

"Honeymoon Mountain martini," he said.

"What's in it?"

"I don't know. Vodka and sweet stuff."

"Can you be a little more specific?"

"Peach? You want some peach. How about some sparkle?"

"That sounds fabulous," she said. "Prepare it for me before you serve it."

"I can do that," he said and winked. "I'll surprise you."

They put the party together in record time, and invitees responded quickly. She barely had a chance to see Benjamin. He seemed to be just as busy in town as she was at the lodge. In fact, the last few nights he'd spent in town. She'd sent him a message inviting him to the party, and he'd sent a text apologizing that he was slammed and couldn't make it. Maybe that was for the best.

She felt edgy and couldn't quite explain why, but she was determined to remain focused. The day of the party, as she dressed, she realized she was late for her period. She wasn't the most regular, but... Vivian couldn't focus on that. She had a party to host.

Walking out in last year's Lilly Pulitzer, she joined Temple and Jillian. Jillian was sparkling like a bright diamond.

Jilly rubbed her hands together. "This is going to be so much fun. I've planned the music," she said.

"Music?" Vivian asked.

Rap sounded from speakers.

"Really?" Temple asked. "You couldn't choose jazz?"

"This is just to get us revved up," Jilly said.

"Or on edge," Temple muttered.

"Stop being a party pooper," Jilly said and pulled Temple into an impromptu dance.

"This isn't my thing," Temple said, awkwardly moving around.

"Stretch yourself," Jilly said. "It'll be good for you."

"Heaven help me," Temple said, but continued to dance.

The doorbell rang, and Jillian clicked the remote. Frank Sinatra oozed through the speakers. "Showtime," she said and pranced toward the front door.

"I want her to represent me at all times," Temple said. "She's so bubbly and friendly. I just want to hide."

"You have your skills," Vivian said. "Don't diminish them."

"If you say so," Temple said. "How are you feeling? You seem a little quiet."

"I'm just getting primed. I'm glad this will last only an afternoon. Getting my smile on," she said.

"Me, too," Temple said, lifting her lips in a grin that was clearly fake and looked more like a grimace.

"You need to work on that. Think of something funny," Vivian said.

"Nothing's funny at the moment," Temple said.

"Then ask someone to tell you a joke," Vivian said. "It's go time."

Despite feeling physically unsettled in a vague way, she marched toward the front door, planted a smile on her face and greeted guests. She chatted and collected business cards in a fishbowl.

Near the end of the open house, a blonde woman approached her. "Hey, I'm Eliza. I didn't get an invitation, but I hope it's okay that I came."

It took a moment before Vivian recognized Benjamin's sister. "Oh, it's lovely to see you again. I'm glad you came. Have you had a bite of our lemon squares or one of our signature drinks?"

"I grabbed a bite of a lemon square. Delicious. I don't drink, though," Eliza said.

"No problem," Vivian said. "We have other beverages."

"I'm okay," Eliza said. "I can see why Benjamin

is fascinated by you. You're beautiful, and you just seem to sparkle."

"You're very kind. Is there something I can do for you?"

"Well, now that you mention it, I have this idea of opening a jewelry and accessory stall at your resort. And I'd like to be a part of it," Eliza said.

"Well, it's a great idea," Vivian said. "But we're not quite ready for anything that specific just yet, since we don't have any definite bookings."

"That's okay," Eliza said. "I just wanted to get my name in during the planning and preparation stage. I think I could offer some cool local jewelry appropriate for your resort."

"I love the idea. I think I have your card, but give it to me again," she said.

"Thanks," Eliza said. "And my brother really likes you. I hope you like him, too."

"I do," Vivian admitted and wished Benjamin had made an appearance at the party. She hadn't seen him in a few days. She wondered what that meant. If anything.

Chapter Eleven

The next morning, Vivian dragged herself from bed. Heavens, she felt so tired. Why?

She started the coffee and literally waited for the machine to produce a cup for her. Sipping despite the fact that it burned her tongue, she wandered to the porch, where Jilly did yoga.

"Want to join me?" Jilly asked, doing some kind of twisty pose.

"I can't even begin to think of it," Vivian said. "I want pastries, coffee and wine. In no particular order."

"Was yesterday that difficult for you?" Jilly asked.

"It's hard to be on all the time. I want this to be a success," Vivian said.

"It's not up to you," Jilly said. "It's part of what the universe provides."

"I can't wait on the universe," Vivian said. "There are people counting on me."

Jilly sighed. "I wish you would be kinder to yourself."

"Me, too," a male voice said from the doorway.

Vivian's heart skipped a beat, and she looked up at Benjamin. "Well, early good morning," she said.

He moved toward her and dropped a kiss on her forehead. "Good morning to you. I'm sorry I couldn't make it yesterday. I'd been away from the bar, and all hell had broken loose with our orders. It took two days to straighten out."

Some part inside her eased. "Thanks," she said.

"I think I'll grab a shower," Jilly said. "Good morning, Benjamin."

"That was lovely and discreet," Vivian said. "Get a cup of coffee for yourself. I'm too lazy to get it for you."

"No worries," Benjamin said and left the porch, then returned with a full mug. He sat down across from her. "So, how did yesterday go?"

"I think pretty well," she said. "It was mostly an invite for the community, but I think we got a few bites for events. Your sister showed up."

His eyes widened. "Oh, really?"

"I wondered if you had told her about the event," she said.

"Not me," he said.

"I was happy to see her. She presented the idea of a jewelry stall. I like the idea. I just can't promise that I can provide her with any ongoing work here," she said.

"That's okay." He frowned. "I don't want you to feel like you need to sell her stuff. She's an artist and—"

Silence stretched between them. "What do you mean?" Vivian asked.

He shrugged. "Her motivation can come and go. But she's very talented."

"Are you saying she's not always consistent?" Vivian asked.

He paused and shrugged again. "Yeah, maybe."

She smiled. "Being consistent is challenging."

"Yeah, but—"

"Yeah, but don't worry about it. I'll do what I can for her. It may not be much, but I'll try."

"Thanks," he said. "So, what's wrong with you?"

"I don't know," she said. "I just feel yucky. I'm hoping it will pass soon."

"Should you see a doctor?" he asked.

"Nah. I'm just a little *off*," she said. "But I need to move past it. I've been invited to an event at the Biltmore Estate celebrating North Carolina tourism next week."

"Me, too," he said. "I heard from them a few weeks ago."

Vivian laughed. "I must be an also-ran. I heard from them this morning."

"They were slow to catch up," he said. "Wanna go with me? Or are you ashamed to be seen with me?"

"Not at all," Vivian said. "You know that was

never the issue. I just didn't want to be hassled by my sisters or anyone else. Like you don't want to be hassled by your sister."

"Fair enough," he said. "We can go separately."

"Let's go together," she said impulsively.

"Are you sure?" he asked.

"Yes," she said. "Why should it be such a big deal?"

"Exactly," he said and leaned toward her to press his lips against hers.

The following week, both Vivian and Benjamin were so busy that they connected only via phone. Vivian still wasn't feeling great, but she tried to push it aside. Her sisters encouraged her to visit a doctor in town, so she made an appointment.

In the meantime, she prepared for the event at the Biltmore by getting a facial and a mani-pedi. She didn't buy a new dress but wore one of her favorite formal dresses. A jade-blue V-neck cocktail dress that highlighted her rosy coloring. She hoped Benjamin would approve.

Temple and Jillian came into her bathroom as she applied last-minute eye makeup.

"More cat eye," Jilly said.

"Less is more," Temple said.

"Line your lips," Jilly said.

"Gloss. Just gloss," Temple corrected her.

Vivian glanced at her sisters, her mascara wand poised. "I'm not sure you're helping."

"You look gorgeous," Jilly said. "I wish I was going."

"I'll pass the next invite to the Biltmore on to you," she said.

"I'm glad it's you and not me," Temple muttered.

Vivian chuckled and gave her eyelashes one last swipe of mascara, then turned around. "I feel like I'm in costume."

"You look like a princess," Jilly said with a huge smile.

"You're very sweet," Vivian said and hugged both her sisters. "I wish I felt better physically."

"You made an appointment with the doctor in town," Temple said.

"Yes. I think I'm just a little worn down."

"It won't hurt to check, although I told you about my yoga and detox regimen. It has worked for me," Jilly said.

"I may ask you more about that after I see the doctor. Just tell me you can't see too many shadows under my eyes," she said.

"None," Jilly said. "Perfect camouflage."

"Thanks. I hope it will last."

The loud doorbell sounded. Vivian felt an excited jiggle in her stomach. "I guess it's time to go."

Both sisters gave her kisses on her cheeks. "That's so sweet," she said, feeling the threat of tears sting her eyes.

"Don't fuss," Temple said. "You're perfect the way you are. Enjoy your evening. Tomorrow you'll be painting and emptying trash."

Vivian chuckled. "Thanks for the reminder. Later, my darlings," she said and swept down the grand staircase. She almost felt like Scarlett O'Hara meeting Rhett Butler, except she was saving a fishing lodge and didn't need his help. He was just as handsome as Rhett, though, she couldn't help thinking.

"I'm almost speechless," Benjamin said. "You are beyond beautiful. Almost as beautiful as you are when your hair is in a ponytail and the only makeup you're wearing is paint."

Vivian sighed. "I think that was the nicest thing you could have said to me."

"It was just the truth," he said and extended his arm. "Shall we go?"

She accepted his arm. "We shall."

It was a magical evening. They traveled to the Biltmore, listening to country music on the way and chatting off and on. She almost forgot that she didn't feel so great physically. As they arrived, the lights of the historic estate greeted them.

"It's beautiful, isn't it?" she asked.

"Nice during the day, too. My school took me for a day trip," he said.

"Really?" she said. "Very cool."

"Did you go to Monticello in Charlottesville?" he asked.

"Of course," she said. "Most school-aged children took a field trip there."

"A few of us lucky ones in Carolina were able to visit Biltmore," he said and pulled up to the valet service. He got out and helped her from her side of his SUV.

"I feel like Cinderella at the ball," she confessed to him.

"I feel almost like a prince," he said, looking deep into her eyes.

"Let's go have a great time," she said.

"We will," he said.

The evening was full of great food, live music and toasts to businesses within the state. Vivian passed out a ton of cards and hoped the contacts would yield returns for Honeymoon Mountain Lodge.

More than that, though, she loved spending the evening with Benjamin. He was so natural. He didn't put on airs. He just displayed his great sense of humor and sly observations.

Soon enough, they needed to leave. Exhausted, Vivian sank back again the seat of his SUV. "What a fabulous night."

"For me, too," he said and dropped a kiss on her lips before he started the drive home.

Vivian drifted off and was embarrassed when she jerked awake as Benjamin pulled to a stop in front of the lodge. He was frowning as his phone rang. He answered it quickly. "Is there a problem? Where is she? I'll be there as soon as possible."

Vivian stared at him and blinked, wondering who *she* was. "What's going on?"

He shook his head. "Sorry. I can't talk about it. I need to go. I'll walk you to the door."

He helped her from the car, clearly distracted.

"What's wrong?" she asked. "I can tell something is wrong. Tell me. Maybe I can help."

"Not this time," he said. "I'm sorry. It was a great evening," he said. "I'll be in touch."

Vivian stared after him, feeling bewildered. She wanted to help him. She sensed he was in pain. At the same time, it hurt that he wouldn't share what was going on with her. Was this about his sister? Vivian was so filled with confusion, she didn't know what to do.

The next morning, Vivian went to the clinic in town. The doctor took a sample of her urine and blood and examined her from head to toe.

"Good news," the cheerful physician's assistant said to her. "You're quite healthy. And pregnant."

Vivian gaped at the woman. "Excuse me?"

"You're pregnant," the PA said. "We need you to start on prenatal vitamins immediately. Otherwise, you're in excellent health."

Still reeling from the PA's announcement, Vivian shook her head. "Excuse me. You're saying I'm pregnant."

"Yes, indeed," the cheerful woman said. "Now, no alcohol intake and continue to exercise. Come in to be evaluated every month. Any questions?" she asked.

"Well," Vivian said.

"Good," the PA said. "Call with any problems," she said and left the room.

Vivian stared after the PA for several moments. A nurse entered the room. "Can I help you?" she asked, probably because Vivian hadn't moved from the examination table.

"It may be too late for that," Vivian said and slid off the table. "Just give me a couple minutes, please."

"Of course. Just let me know if you need my help," the nurse said.

Vivian dressed and walked slowly from the room. Had she just had an out-of-body experience? Was she really pregnant? She stopped by the exit window.

"Here's a small quantity of prenatal vitamins to get you started," the clerk said and stripped off a piece of paper from a pad. "Here's your prescription for the rest of them. If you need a laxative, let us know. These things can stop you up. Congrats and good luck," the woman said.

"Thank you very much," Vivian said, completely dismayed.

She walked outside the clinic, the sun glaring down on her. Well, what to do next? She was a modern woman. She knew she had options. She would keep this baby. The question was, would she raise it with or without Benjamin's assistance?

Vivian arrived back at the lodge with a plan in mind. As soon as she entered the door, Temple greeted her. "So, did you find out what's wrong?"

"I need some vitamins," Vivian said. "I'm a little low on a few of them."

"So they gave you a script?" Temple asked.

"They did," Vivian said.

"Good," Temple said. "In the meantime, the phone has been ringing off the hook here. Apparently people are all worked up after our party last week and your visit to the Biltmore."

"Do any of them want to hold events here?" Vivian asked.

"I sure hope so," Temple said. "We need customers."

"I'll get right on it," Vivian said.

Temple caught her arm. "Take a nap if that's what you need," she said. "You're still looking a little tired."

Vivian pulled her sister against her for a big hug. "Thanks. Love you."

Temple squeezed her, then pulled back in surprise. "Are you sure you're okay?"

"I'm fine. I'll be fine. I'm all about fine," Vivian said.

"That sounds a little too fine," Temple said.

"Don't question me," Vivian said.

"Okay," Temple said. "No questions. Just take your vitamins, please."

Vivian spent the rest of the day following up on calls. She had several big bites of interest for events at the lodge. Thank goodness, because she still hadn't heard from Corinne Whitman Jergenson, and she was losing hope.

The next morning Vivian dragged herself out of bed, and it took all of her concentration to keep from getting sick to her stomach. She crept to the kitchen, popped open a can of ginger ale and grabbed some crackers. This kinda sucked, she thought. She felt a measure of sympathy for her mother. After all, she had gone through this three times.

Vivian wanted to get in touch with Benjamin, but he had been absent recently. Taking deep breaths and sipping soda, she returned to her room and called potential clients.

Halfway through the day, a knock sounded at the door. She opened it to Temple. "What's up?"

"Mother," Temple said, her eyes wide, her skin pale.

"What do you mean, Mother?" Vivian asked.

"She is here," Temple said in a stilted voice.

Vivian muttered a series of swearwords she never, ever used. "I'll be right out," she said and grabbed her glass of soda and a cracker.

Taking a deep breath, she walked to the living room and nodded toward her spotless, stunning mother.

"Hello, Mother. How are you?" she asked.

Tinsley Ferguson stood in all her stiffly perfect auburn glory and looked at Vivian for a long moment. "You're pregnant, aren't you?"

Vivian silently gaped at her mother.

"Cracker, soda," her mother said. "I've lived through this three times. Who's the father? And why couldn't you make it work with your husband?"

"I couldn't make it work with my ex because he knocked up someone else while we were married," she said. "But I've already explained that to you. To what do we owe the honor of your visit?" she asked in her most Tinsley voice ever.

Her mother lifted both her eyebrows, which was quite a feat given all the wrinkle filler injected in her brows. "I've heard about your endeavors with the lodge. Corinne Whitman Jergenson contacted me."

"I'm sure you recommended us," Vivian said.

"Well, I was quite surprised that all of you were involved. Where is Jillian?"

"I hope in yogaland," Temple muttered.

Her mother shot Temple a sharp glance. "You haven't shown yourself in Richmond for ages," she said.

"It's not her sparkle place," Jilly said as she entered the room. "Hello, Mommy."

Vivian instinctively moved between Jilly and her mother. "Jilly, Mom made a surprise visit."

"We're so lucky," Temple muttered.

Jilly stepped in front of Vivian. "Hello, Mommy. How are you doing?"

"Well. And you?"

"I'm thrilled to be reunited with my sisters," Jilly said. "I've missed them."

"Hmm," Tinsley said.

"And you," Jilly said.

Mother blinked. "I'm quite fine. It's a surprise to see you again."

"Yes. And you should know that I'll never be what you wanted me to be," Jilly blurted out.

Tinsley bit her lip. "I've had some time to think about that. Maybe I'm okay with that."

"Maybe?" Jilly asked, crossing her arms over her chest.

Vivian held her breath. She had pictured this meeting, but in her imagination, it had never gone this way.

Mom took a deep breath. "I am okay with that. It's hard because I always wanted the best for all of you."

"But what you want may not match up with what we want or need," Vivian said as gently as she could because her mother seemed almost more vulnerable than Jilly was.

"I know. It's still difficult for me, but I've missed you all so much. I just don't want us to be so separate from each other anymore."

"I have tattoos," Jilly said.

Tinsley cringed. "Okay. Just please don't show them to me."

Jilly chuckled and raced toward their mother. She embraced her. "I've missed you, Mommy."

"I've missed you, too," Tinsley said. She opened her arms to Temple and Vivian. "Please let me hug you."

Temple and Vivian walked into their mother's loving arms. Vivian's heart overflowed with emotion. She'd never thought this kind of reunion was possible.

"Vivian," her mother said. "You must tell me who got you knocked up. I'll make sure he will pay."

"Oh, Mom, I'm vitamin deficient. Really," Vivian said. "I tested yesterday. I need to beef up my vitamins."

"Really?" her mother said skeptically. "You look tired and bloated to me."

"Well, thank you very much," Vivian said. "You look like you've had a little too much filler."

Her mother lifted her chin in disapproval. "That's entirely inappropriate."

"As is your comment about me looking bloated," Vivian said.

Her mother pursed her lips. "Well, perhaps it was. Shall we have some tea, lemonade or bourbon or all of that?"

"All of that sounds good to me," Temple said.

Chapter Twelve

After a full day with her mother on site, Vivian brushed her teeth and sank down onto her bed. Her stomach was churning. She supposed this was what she should expect for the next few months. As she rested her head on her pillow, she wondered how she would tell Benjamin.

A knock sounded on her door. "Yes?" Vivian said but didn't rise.

Temple stepped inside her room. "I know you're pregnant."

"No. I'm not."

"Yes, you are. But I want you to know that I will be here for you. Even through birthing and delivery, as long you promise to get an epidural."

"Well, thank you very much," Vivian said, opening her arms to her sister. "Just so you know, I am in a full state of denial with Mom."

"Good luck, and I'll fib with you until the bloody end," Temple said, squeezing her tight. "Have you told Benjamin?"

"Not yet," Vivian said.

"It will all be okay," Temple said and stroked Vivian's forehead.

"How can you be sure?" Vivian asked.

"You picked an excellent man," Temple said.

"But what if he doesn't really love me?"

Temple chuckled. "He did a long, long time ago."

"I hope that's at least partly true," Vivian said, but she needed to see Benjamin. She needed to tell him. "I've tried calling him, but he hasn't returned my call yet. I don't want to appear desperate."

"Well, this is pretty important. Knowing you, you told him, 'Get in touch with me when you can,' which doesn't sound like the topic is pressing."

Pretty close, Vivian thought. "I'll wait until tonight. Maybe there's something big going on at the bar, or he's buying a new business. He mentioned something about that lately."

"Don't wait too long," Temple said and dropped a kiss on Vivian's forehead. "Sleep well. You need it."

Vivian waited and debated calling that night. Instead, she decided to try to sleep. When she awakened in the morning, though, and struggled with nausea, she knew it was time to talk to Benjamin. Today she would go into town.

* * *

Benjamin had barely been able to return to the bar for more than thirty minutes during the last couple of days. His sister had been on suicide watch, and he'd known he needed to stay with her as much as possible. She'd run out of her medicine and had hoped she could manage on her own. She'd done the same thing several times prior. He wished she could find and accept the help she needed. The side effects of her medication sometimes made her quit it altogether.

Despite the fact that it was midday, he was so tired he could barely put one foot in front of the other. In his office, he studied spreadsheets and order forms.

A knock sounded at the door. He lifted his head. "Yes? Come on in."

Vivian appeared in the doorway with a questioning look on her face. "Everything okay?"

"Not really," he said and rubbed his hand over his face. "I'm sorry I haven't called you back. I've been tied up."

She gave a slow nod. "New business you're purchasing?"

"No. Not that." He sighed. A long silence followed. "I can't talk about it."

"Oh," she said. "Okay. Well, I need to talk to you."

He closed his laptop. "That's fine. You want to close the door behind you?"

"Yes. I think that's a good idea," she said, pushing the door shut and standing in front of his desk.

"You want to sit down?"

She crossed her arms over her chest. "Not really."

Benjamin felt a strange twist in his gut. What was going on? "Okay. I'm all ears."

She bit her lip. "Well. I'm pregnant."

Benjamin stared at her for several seconds, unable to comprehend her words. "Excuse me?"

"I'm. Pregnant."

Benjamin blinked and glanced down. "Wow. I—uh—I—"

"It caught me by surprise, too," she said. "I didn't think I was particularly fertile because—" She broke off and shook her head. "Well, I just didn't. But I really thought you should know."

"Yes, I should," he said, his mind reeling. How had this happened? He'd used protection. What if this baby also suffered from mental health? He should reveal that to Vivian.

"I thought I should tell you," she said and turned as if she planned to leave.

"Wait," he said, standing. His integrity rose inside him. "I'll be here for you and for the baby."

Her face seemed to fall. "That's good to know," she said in an ultrapolite voice. "I guess I'll see you later."

Benjamin frowned as she left his office. He was still whirling from the news. How had this happened? Of course he knew how it had happened, and he had enjoyed every minute. But…

His mind still slamming from one prospect to another, he raced from the office and caught up with Vivian as she walked toward her car. "Hey," he called and took her hand. "Wait up."

She turned to look at him. "What?"

"We should get married. If we're going to have a baby, you and I should get married."

She stared at him for a long moment and bit her lip. "Is that a proposal?"

"Yeah," he said and smiled, feeling elated at the prospect. "Yeah, I guess it is."

"You think we *should* get married," she said. "I have no interest in a *should* marriage. I've already had a bad marriage. I don't want another one," she said, pulled her hand from his and walked away.

"Wait," he said. "How do you know it would be bad?"

"I don't know much, but starting out with a big *should* isn't good. Thanks for the offer, but no thanks," she said and walked to her car.

Benjamin stared after her, knowing in his gut that he had done everything wrong. He wasn't sure how to fix it. He wondered if he possibly could fix it. His prospects sure didn't look good at the moment.

Vivian's mother had to leave the following day. Thank goodness. Her mother frowned at her.

"Are you sure you're not pregnant? You look a bit green," her mother said.

"No chance," Vivian said, nibbling on a muffin she didn't want.

"Are you sure you haven't been exposed?" her mother asked with a slight smirk.

"Oh, Mother," Vivian said.

Temple entered the room with a yawn. "We may as well be in a convent. No need to worry about us."

"Hmm," her mother said. "Well, I must say the lodge is much nicer than I remembered. I think I'll pass along recommendations to some of my friends."

"Oh, please. Don't feel obligated," Vivian said.

"I'm okay if you do," Temple said.

Jilly poured a cup of coffee and offered it to her mother. "Do what makes you feel whole," she said. "Nothing more. Nothing less."

Their mother stared at Jilly. "I'm not sure how I gave birth to you or how you have any DNA from your father or me, but I'm very glad that you're here and I've gotten the opportunity to see you. I want all of you to come to Richmond to visit."

"Absolutely," Jilly said.

"That sounds lovely," Vivian said.

"And you can come here anytime you like," Jilly said.

"Thank you for visiting, Mother," Vivian said and brushed her mother's cheek with a light kiss.

Temple did the same.

Jilly flung her arms around their mother and pressed her pink lips against her mother's cheek. "Thanks for coming, Mommy."

Their mother blinked. "Well, you're very welcome. I'll be in touch, darlings. Ta-ta," she said and started for the door. "Oh, would one of you bring my luggage to my car? It's a bit much for me."

Jilly eagerly stepped forward for the task.

For the rest of the day, Vivian was torn between worrying about Jilly's hopes for a wonderful relationship with their mother and her own pregnancy. Temple had asked about Vivian's trip into town, but Vivian had waved her aside. She hadn't known what she'd expected from Benjamin, but she knew she hadn't gotten what she'd hoped.

She spent the day sitting on the screened-in porch and updating the website, and Benjamin appeared in the late afternoon. "Hey, there," he said. "I really messed up yesterday, didn't I?"

"You were caught off guard. I was, too," she said, feeling her muscles tighten into hard knots.

"You're being kind," he said, stepping in front of her, his hands shoved in his pockets. "I talked about marriage, but I didn't talk about our feelings for each other."

She took a quick, sharp breath and closed her eyes. Vivian couldn't think about feelings. Her feelings overwhelmed her. She shrugged. "It's okay. It's—"

He sank down beside her and took her hands. "It's not okay," he said. "We've been drawn to each other. This baby happened for a reason. This baby happened because we love each other, because we want a future together."

His words blindsided her, and she searched his

face. *Love?* "What are you saying? What are you feeling?"

"I love you," he confessed. "I think I've loved you for a long time. Longer than I would admit to myself."

She bit her lip. "Are you sure?"

He nodded. "Yes, I'm—" His cell phone rang and he glanced at it. He swore. "I have to take this. I'm really sorry."

He rose from the couch and stepped away.

She couldn't hear what he was saying and felt frustrated by the interruption. What could be so important?

A moment later, he reentered the porch. "I'm sorry. I had to take that."

"What was *that*?" she asked. "What was so important that you couldn't share it with me? How can we get married if you are going to keep things from me? Important things?"

He took a deep breath. "I gave my word to my sister. I need to talk to her about this."

"Sister?" she echoed.

"Yeah. Sister," he said. "Give me a day. It's important."

"I hope she's okay," Vivian said.

"I'm always hoping for that," he said. He paused a half beat, then pressed a hard kiss against her mouth. "Don't count me out."

Her heart was slamming against her chest. How could she?

* * *

The following day, she awakened and lost her cookies. This whole pregnancy was getting real as each day passed. She needed to toughen up. She had months to go. Oh, wait. And years after that.

Fighting off anxiety attacks, she took deep breaths and drank decaf tea. Sipping a cup, she sat on the porch. Jilly sat down beside her. "I can tell you're upset. How can I help you?"

Vivian looked at her sweet bleach-blonde sister, dressed in yoga capris and a tank top, and felt love swell in her heart. "I'm good. It just makes me happy that you are here. But if you need to leave, I'll understand. This isn't a sure deal."

Jilly laughed. "Most of my deals haven't been sure, but now I have a roof over my head, and I get to be with my sisters. My life couldn't be much better."

"I need to warn you that Mom can be a little inconsistent," Vivian said. "I don't know how to say this because your relationship with her may be different."

Jilly nodded earnestly. "She's a bit of a wench, isn't she? I wonder what made her that way."

Vivian tilted her head to one side. "I never thought about it that way. I just don't want you to be hurt."

Jilly smiled. "That's one of the nicest things someone has said to me in a long time."

Vivian smiled, too. "I'm so glad we've reconnected. I just really want you to be careful."

"I will be okay. She has rejected me several times before. I'm stronger because of it," Jilly said.

"I can see that," Vivian said, seeing a spark of strength in her sister's eyes. Maybe she could trust Jilly to set her own boundaries.

"But I'm concerned about you," Jilly said. "I sense something has changed about you."

"Your sense is correct," Vivian said. "But I'd rather talk about it at a different time. Is that okay?"

"You've made me even more curious, but I guess I'll have to wait. I'm wondering if Mommy was right about you being pregnant," Jilly said.

"Can we talk about something else?" Vivian asked.

Later that night, her cell phone rang. She hadn't found the energy to shower, so she just lay on her back on the bed with her eyes half-closed.

Not looking at the caller ID, she automatically said, "Vivian Jackson. Hello."

"Hello to you," Benjamin said.

Vivian's eyes flew open, and she sat up in her bed. "Hello," she repeated. Then she stuttered, "H-how are things?"

"Could be better. Could be worse," he said. "Any chance you can come to the county hospital?"

Vivian blinked. "Umm. Sure. When?"

"Now," he said.

She swallowed over her surprise. "Now?"

"Yeah, Eliza may need to be moved to another facility," he said.

"Oh, no. Has she been injured?" she asked.

"It's complicated," he said. "Can you come?"

"Yes," she said without pausing. "I'll be there as soon as I can."

She got up, brushed her teeth and rubbed the dark makeup from under her eyes. Her mother would be horrified. Thank goodness her mother wasn't here.

Walking out her door, she ran into both of her sisters.

Temple, dressed in jammies and carrying a brownie, looked at her. "Where are you going?"

"Benjamin called. He wants me to meet him at the county hospital."

"Oh, no," Jilly said, also wearing her jammies. "Is he okay?"

"I think he is. Mostly," Vivian said.

Temple frowned. "Then what's wrong?"

Vivian hesitated. "Please don't spread it around, but I think it's about his sister, Eliza."

"Oh," Jilly said. "Please call us and let us know. She seemed nice and talented."

"Drive safely," Temple said. "Should I drive for you?"

"I'm good," Vivian said and shrugged. "Just think good thoughts."

Heading out the door, she got into her car and drove to the county hospital, worrying and wondering all the way. She pulled into the parking lot, went to the front desk and asked for Eliza Hunter.

The attendant seemed a bit reluctant to release any information. "And who are you?" she asked.

"Vivian Jackson," she said.

The attendant gave a slow nod. "She's on the fourth floor. You'll have to check in at the desk."

"Thank you," Vivian said, wondering and worrying even more as she walked into the elevator and punched the button for the fourth floor.

The elevator door opened, and she walked to the desk. "I'm here to see Eliza Hunter," she said.

"Just a moment, please," the attendant said and turned away from her.

Vivian waited. And waited.

"Ms. Hunter's brother will be out to meet you," she said.

A few seconds later, Benjamin appeared.

"What's going on?" Vivian asked.

"It's complicated, but Eliza wants to explain," he said.

Vivian frowned. "Eliza? Why can't you explain?"

He shrugged. "I made a promise. This is a big moment for her."

Vivian took a deep breath. "Okay. I hope she's well."

"We're working on it," he said and led her down the hallway. They entered a room where Eliza lay in a bed with her arms tied to the rails.

She glanced up weakly. "Hi, there," she said.

"Hi," Vivian said, moving quickly to the side of the bed. "Are you okay?"

"I will be," Eliza said. "I stopped taking my medication. I keep hoping I won't need it." She bit her lip. "And then I get depressed. Very depressed."

"I'm so sorry," Vivian said and reached out to touch Eliza.

Eliza glanced up at Benjamin. "I think you got a good one," she said, then turned to Vivian. "I'm bipolar. I didn't want Benjamin to tell you or anyone, but I think, maybe, it's time for me to stop being so secretive."

"Oh, Eliza, I'm so sorry," Vivian said. "You shouldn't suffer this alone! It's terrible for you and anyone you love," she said. "But your disease is like diabetes. You need daily treatment. You need a support group." She shrugged. "I'm sorry you have struggled with this, and maybe you'll always struggle in a way, but you must accept assistance for yourself and Benjamin."

Eliza's chin sank to her chest. "Why is this so hard?"

Vivian shook her head. "I bet you've tried to do too much on your own. All of us need help at times. All of us," she said.

Eliza stared into her eyes. "I've just always felt ashamed."

"There are far worse things. You have so many strengths. You are creative, loving and friendly. The world is blessed by your presence."

Eliza's eyes filled with tears. "I don't know what to say."

"Say you'll be more gentle with yourself," Vivian told her.

Eliza closed her eyes as tears streamed down her

cheeks. "Am I ever going to get over this?" she whispered.

Vivian's heart nearly broke at Eliza's suffering. "I'm not telling you anything you don't know. I suspect it's day by day. And you bring light and pleasure to many people. You just need to allow yourself to bring light and pleasure to yourself. You need to remember that you are quite wonderful. Remembering that every day may take some doing."

"How do you know all this?" Eliza asked.

"I've had friends who struggled with this disease and I've had more than a few moments of self-doubt myself. My life hasn't been perfect," Vivian confessed.

"But you know Benjamin wants to marry you," Eliza said.

Vivian's breath caught in her throat. "We're working on that."

"He's been here with me the last few days. I made him swear he wouldn't tell anyone what was going on with me," she said.

Vivian looked at Benjamin. "That explains a lot."

"I wanted to keep my word," he said. "That's why I brought you here tonight."

She stared into his eyes and saw love, love, love. "We need to talk," she said.

"Tell me the news when it happens," Eliza said. "I'm going into a mental health facility, so I'll be out of touch for a while."

Vivian squeezed Eliza's hand. "Good for you. I'm proud of you," she said.

Eliza shrugged. "It will be a lot of work. Not my first rodeo, but I'm ready for this step."

Vivian stepped closer and kissed Eliza on her cheek. "Call me anytime," she said.

Benjamin did the same. "Thank you for tonight," he said.

"It was the least I could do. Gonna give your baby my middle name?" Eliza asked.

Vivian gaped at Benjamin, and he shrugged.

"I had to tell her. I had to stop keeping secrets from you and from her," he said.

Vivian nodded in understanding. "When can we talk?" she asked.

"In just a few minutes. They're going to limit my visits so she can focus on her treatment."

"I'll wait outside," Vivian said.

Vivian paced in the empty waiting room, her emotions roiling.

Benjamin approached her.

"Do you think she'll be okay?" Vivian asked.

"With proper help and medication, she always comes out of this. It can be a terrifying ride, but I think she would do much better if she would join a support group and stick with it. I haven't had much luck convincing her."

Vivian inhaled, trying to collect her thoughts. "You shouldn't have kept this from me," she said.

"I gave my word to Eliza," he said.

"Well, you should have convinced her to release you from that promise. It's wrong for you to suffer this alone. What if I had kept something like this from you?"

He shook his head. "Totally unacceptable."

"That's the way I feel about you. I thought we had something special, but—"

"We do," he said putting his hands on her arms. "We do. I'm just not used to sharing the load when it comes to Eliza. Even the idea is new to me."

"I may not seem like I'm strong enough to handle this kind of thing, but—"

"I never thought that," he said. "I just thought you might not be interested. Not everyone would be."

"Well, of course, I'm interested. Eliza is an important part of your life. She's precious to you so she would also be precious to me."

Benjamin shook his head in disbelief. "I can't believe I found you. I can't believe you're here right now. You're the strongest, most caring, most fascinating woman I've ever met, and I want you in my life. Forever," he said. "I love you."

The commitment in his words vibrated through her. She could hear and feel the certainty, but a part of her was afraid to believe. "Are you sure?" she asked. "This has happened pretty fast. Are you sure you're not saying this because of the baby?"

"I couldn't be more sure," Benjamin said and took a deep breath. "But maybe you need some time."

Vivian blinked. Sure, she had vacillated at the beginning. Her feelings had been so strong even then. But now, and not just because of the baby, she wanted him more than ever. She wanted his presence in her life. She wanted to be there for him and for him to be there for her. She checked herself. Her heart, mind and soul all agreed. She knew that being with him was right.

"I love you. I've never known a man I trust more. That I love being with more. We've had some tricky moments. Some fun and some scary ones. Life is like that. You're the one I want to be with through all those times."

He shook his head. "I don't even have a ring for you."

"I'd rather have your heart forever," she said, and he lowered his mouth to hers in a kiss that promised everything.

Epilogue

Three weeks and two days later, the first wedding at Honeymoon Mountain Lodge was held between Benjamin and Vivian. Another wedding was scheduled in two weeks. That was the wedding of Corinne Whitman Jergenson's daughter, Olive, and her groom, Bubba.

Vivian and Benjamin had wanted to wait until his sister was out of the mental health facility so that all their important people could join them. The weather was gorgeous, and although the leaves were falling, the clear blue lake provided a beautiful backdrop for the vows they would take on the dock.

The wedding crowd was small with no attendants. Vivian took one last glance in the mirror and walked down the hallway to where her sisters and mother stood.

"You look beautiful," Jilly said.

"You do," Temple said. "Are you sure you want to go through with this? I mean, marriage is challenging."

Their mother shot Temple a sharp glance. "Of course she does. She's pregnant."

Vivian shook her head. "Of course. I do. I love Benjamin and he loves me. Y'all go ahead. I want a moment."

Her sisters and mother exited to the dock, and Vivian closed her eyes. "Well, Daddy, all I can say is thank you for leaving the lodge to us and introducing me to the love of my life. I hope you're happy up there. We sure miss you," she whispered and felt her eyes well with tears.

Blinking furiously to dry her eyes, she walked to the door, which Grayson opened for her. His eyes turned a bit shiny. "You look beautiful, Missy. Your father would be proud."

The strains of a guitar played, and Vivian looked to the front of the small group where Benjamin stood.

Dressed in a dark suit, he looked more handsome than ever. His gaze locked with hers, and he broke tradition by rushing to meet her and pulling her against him. "I love you so much," he said.

"I was thinking the same thing about you," she said and joined him as they walked to the front, where the minister stood waiting. She heard a few whispers but couldn't make out what was said.

She stared into Benjamin's gaze as they repeated their vows. They might have taken the long road to finding each other again, but it had been worth it.

"I now pronounce you husband and wife," the minister said.

Benjamin swooped her up in his arms and kissed her.

The crowd laughed and cheered.

"I knew she was pregnant," her mother said to Temple as she wiped her eyes. "A mother knows these things."

"She looks so beautiful," Jilly said.

"They are so happy," Eliza said.

And nothing else needed to be said, because it was true. Benjamin and Vivian were so happy, at last.

* * * * *

Looking for more Leanne Banks?
Try her other romantic stories:

A PRINCESS UNDER THE MISTLETOE
A ROYAL CHRISTMAS PROPOSAL
MAVERICK FOR HIRE
HAPPY NEW YEAR, BABY FORTUNE!
THE MAVERICK & THE MANHATTANITE

Available now from Harlequin Special Edition!

Pretending they're lovers for the cameras on a reality TV show quickly has Travis Dalton and Brenna O'Reilly wishing this game of love would never have to end...

Turn the page for a sneak preview of New York Times *bestselling author* Christine Rimmer's

THE MAVERICK FAKES A BRIDE!,

the first book in the next Montana Mavericks *continuity,*

MONTANA MAVERICKS:
THE GREAT FAMILY ROUNDUP

Chapter One

Early March, Rust Creek Falls, Montana

It was a warm day for March. And everyone in Bee's Beauty Parlor that afternoon had gathered at the wide front windows to watch as Travis Dalton rode his favorite bay gelding down Broomtail Road.

The guy was every cowgirl's fantasy in a snug Western shirt, butt-hugging jeans, Tony Lama boots and a black hat. One of those film school graduates from the little theater in nearby Kalispell, a video camera stuck to his face, walked backward ahead of him, recording his every move. Travis talked and gestured broadly as he went.

"My, my, my." Bee smoothed her brassy blond hair, though it didn't need it. Even in a high wind,

Bee's hair never moved. "Travis does have one fine seat on a horse."

There were soft, low sounds of agreement and appreciation from the women at the window—and then, out of nowhere, Travis tossed his hat in the air and flipped to a handstand right there on that horse in the middle of the street.

The women applauded. There was more than one outright cry of delight.

Only Brenna O'Reilly stood still and silent. She had her arms wrapped around her middle to keep from clapping, and she'd firmly tucked her lips between her teeth in order not to let out a single sound.

Because no way was Brenna sighing over Travis Dalton. Yes, he was one hot cowboy, with that almost-black hair and those dangerous blue eyes, that hard, lean body, and that grin that could make a girl's lady parts spontaneously combust.

And it wasn't only his looks that worked for her. Sometimes an adventurous woman needed a hero on hand. Travis had come to her rescue more than once in her life.

But he'd always made a big deal about how he was too old for her—and okay, maybe he'd had a point, back when she was six and he was fourteen. But now that she'd reached the grown-up age of twenty-six, what did eight years even matter?

Never mind. Not going to happen, Brenna reminded herself for the ten thousandth time. And no matter what people in town might say, she was not and never had been in love with the man.

Right now, today, she was simply appreciating the view, which was spectacular.

Beside her, Dovey Jukes actually let out a moan and made a big show of fanning herself. "Is it just me, or is it *really* hot in here?"

"This is his, er, what did you call it now, Melba?" Bee asked old Melba Strickland, who'd come out from under the dryer to watch the local heartthrob ride by.

"It's his package," replied Melba.

Dovey snickered.

Bee let out her trademark smoke-and-whiskey laugh. "Not *that* kind of package." She gave Dovey a playful slap on the arm.

"It's reality television slang," Melba clarified. "Tessa told me all about it." Melba's granddaughter lived in Los Angeles now. Tessa Strickland Drake had a high-powered job in advertising and understood how things worked in the entertainment industry. "A package is an audition application and video."

"Audition for what?" one of the other girls asked.

"A brand-new reality show." Melba was in the know. "It's going to get made at a secret location right here in Montana this summer, and it will be called *The Great Roundup*. From what I heard, it's going to be like *Survivor*, but with cowboys—you know, roping and branding, bringing in the strays, everyone sharing their life stories around the campfire, sleeping out under the stars, answering challenge after challenge, trying not to get eliminated. The winner will earn himself a million-dollar prize."

Brenna, who'd never met a challenge she couldn't rise to, clutched the round thermal brush in her hand a little tighter and tried to ignore the tug of longing in heart. After all, she'd been raised on the family ranch and could rope and ride with the best of them. She couldn't help but imagine herself on this new cowboy reality show.

True, lately, she'd been putting in some serious effort to quell her wild and crazy side, to settle down a little, you might say.

But a reality show? She could enjoy the excitement while accomplishing a valid goal of winning those big bucks. A few months ago, Bee had started dating a handsome sixtyish widower from Kalispell. Now that things had gotten serious, she'd been talking about selling the shop and retiring so she and her new man could travel. Brenna would love to step up as owner when Bee left.

But that would cost money she didn't have. If she won a million dollars on a reality show, however, she could buy the shop and still have plenty of money to spare.

And then again, no. Trying out for a reality show was a crazy idea, and Brenna was keeping a lid on her wild side, she truly was. *The Great Roundup* was not for her.

She asked wistfully, "You think Travis has a chance to be on the show?"

"Are you kidding?" Bee let out a teasing growl. "Those Hollywood people would be crazy not to choose him. And if the one doing the choosing is female, all that man has to do is give her a smile."

Every woman at that window enthusiastically agreed.

First week of May, a studio soundstage, Los Angeles, California

Travis Dalton hooked his booted foot across his knee and relaxed in the interview chair.

It was happening. *Really* happening. His video had wowed them. And his application? He'd broken all the rules with it, just like that book he'd bought—*Be a Reality Star*—had instructed. He'd used red ink, added lots of silly Western doodles and filled it chock-full of colorful stories of his life on the family ranch.

He'd knocked them clean out of their boots, if he did say so himself. And now here he was in Hollywood auditioning for *The Great Roundup*.

"Tell us about growing up on a ranch," said the casting director, whose name was Giselle. Giselle dressed like a fashion model. She had a way of making a guy feel like she could see inside his head. *Sharp*. That was the word for Giselle. Sharp—and interested. Her calculating eyes watched him so closely.

Which was fine. Good. He wanted her looking at him with interest. He wanted to make the cut, get on *The Great Roundup* and win himself a million bucks.

Travis gave a slow grin in the general direction of one of the cameras that recorded every move he made. "I grew up on my family's ranch in northwestern Montana." He was careful to include Giselle's question in his answer, in case they ended up using this interview in the show. Then they could cut Giselle's voice out and what he said would still make perfect sense. "My dad put me on a horse for the first time at the age of five. Sometimes it feels like I was born in the saddle."

Giselle and her assistant nodded their approval as he went on—about the horses he'd trained and the ones that had thrown him. About the local rodeos where he'd been bucked off more than one bad-tempered bull—and made it all the way to eight full seconds on a few. He thought it was going pretty well, that he was charming them, winning them over, showing them he wasn't shy, that an audience would love him.

"Can you take off your shirt for us, Travis?"

He'd assumed that would be coming. Rising, Travis unbuttoned and shrugged out of his shirt. At first, he kept it all business, no funny stuff. They needed to get a good look at the body that ranching had built and he kept in shape. He figured they wouldn't be disappointed.

But they wanted to see a little personality, too, so when Giselle instructed, "Turn around slowly," he held out his arms, bending his elbows and bringing them down, giving them the cowboy version of a bodybuilder's flex. As he turned, he grabbed his hat off the back of his chair and plunked it on his head, aiming his chin to the side, giving them a profile shot and then going all the way with a slow grin and a wink over his shoulder.

The casting assistant, Roxanne, stifled a giggle as she grinned right back.

"Go ahead and sit back down," Giselle said. She wasn't flirty like Roxanne, but in her sharp-edged way she seemed happy with how the interview was shaking out.

Travis took off his hat again. He bent to get his shirt.

"Leave it," said Giselle.

He gave her a slight nod and no smile as he settled back into the chair. Because this was serious business. To him—and to her.

"Now we want to know about that hometown of yours." Giselle almost smiled then, though really it was more of a smirk. "We've been hearing some pretty crazy things about Rust Creek Falls."

Was he ready for that one? You bet he was. His town had been making national news the past few years. First came the flood. He explained about the Fourth of July rains that wouldn't stop and all the ways the people of Rust Creek Falls had pulled together to come back from the worst disaster in a century. He spoke of rebuilding after the waters receded, of the national attention and the sudden influx of young women who had come to town to find themselves a cowboy.

When Giselle asked if any of those women had

found him, he answered in a lazy drawl, "To tell you the truth, I met a lot of pretty women after the great flood." He put his right hand on his chest. "Each one of them holds a special place in my heart."

Roxanne had to stifle another giggle.

Giselle sent her a cool look. Roxanne's smile vanished as if it had never been. "Tell us more," said Giselle.

And he told them about a certain Fourth of July wedding almost two years ago now, a wedding in Rust Creek Falls Park. A local eccentric by the name of Homer Gilmore had spiked the wedding punch with his special recipe moonshine—purported to make people do things they would never do ordinarily.

"A few got in fights," he confessed, "present company included, I'm sorry to say." He made an effort to look appropriately embarrassed at his own behavior before adding, "And a whole bunch of folks got romantic—and that meant that *last* year, Rust Creek Falls had a serious baby boom. You might have heard of that. We called it the baby bonanza. So now we have what amounts to a population explosion in our little town. Nobody's complaining, though. In Rust Creek Falls, love and babies are what it's all about."

Travis explained that he wanted to join the cast of *The Great Roundup* for the thrill of it—and he also wanted to be the last cowboy standing. He had a fine life working the Dalton family ranch, but the million-dollar prize would build him his own house on the land he loved and put a little money in the bank, too.

"I'm not getting any younger," he admitted with a smile he hoped came across as both sexy *and* modest. "One of these days, I might even want to find the right girl and settle down."

Giselle, who had excellent posture in the first place, seemed to sit up even straighter, like a prize hunting dog catching a scent. "The right girl? Interesting." She glanced at Roxanne, who bobbed her head in an eager nod. "Is there anyone special you've got your eye on?"

There was no one, and there probably wouldn't be any time soon. But he got Giselle's message loud and clear. For some reason, the casting director would prefer that he had a sweetheart.

And what Giselle preferred, Travis Dalton was bound and determined to deliver. "Is there a special woman in my life? Well, she's a...very private person."

"That would be yes, then. You're exclusive with someone?"

Damn. Message received, loud and clear. He wasn't getting out of this without confessing—or lying through his teeth. And since he intended to get on the show, he knew what his choice had to be.

"I don't want to speak out of hand, but yeah. There is a special someone in my life now. We...haven't been together long, but..." He let out a low whistle and pasted on an expression that he hoped would pass for completely smitten. "Oh, yeah. *Special* would be the word for her."

"Is this special someone a hometown girl?" Giselle's eyes twinkled in a way that was simultaneously aggressive, gleeful and calculating.

"She's from Rust Creek Falls, yes. And she's amazing." *Whoever the hell she is.* "It's the greatest thing in the world, to know someone your whole life and then suddenly to realize there's a lot more going on between the two of you than you've ever admitted before." Whoa. He probably ought to be ashamed of himself. His mama had brought him up right, taught him not to tell lies. But who did this little white lie hurt, anyway? Not a soul. And to get on *The Great Roundup*, Travis Dalton would tell Giselle whatever she needed to hear.

"What's her name?" asked Giselle. It was the next logical question, damn it. He should have known it was coming.

He put on his best killer smile—and lied some more. "Sorry, I can't tell you her name. You know small towns." Giselle frowned. She might be sharp as a barbwire fence, but he would bet his Collin Traub dress saddle that she'd never been within a hundred miles of a town like Rust Creek Falls. "We're keeping what we have together just between the two of us, my girl and me. It's a special time in our relationship, and we don't want the whole town butting into our private business." *A special time.* Damned if he didn't sound downright sensitive—

for a bald-faced liar. But would the casting director buy it?

Giselle didn't seem all that thrilled with his un-
willingness to out his nonexistent girlfriend, but at
least she let it go. A few minutes later, she gave the
cameraman a break. Then she chatted with Travis
off the record for a couple of minutes more. She said
she'd heard he was staying at the Malibu house of
LA power player Carson Drake, whose wife, Tessa
Strickland Drake, had deep Montana roots. Travis
explained that he'd known Tessa all his life. She'd
grown up in Bozeman, but she spent most of her
childhood summers staying at her grandmother's
boardinghouse in Rust Creek Falls.

After the chitchat, Giselle asked him to have a
seat outside. He grabbed his shirt and went out to the
waiting area, which consisted of a bunch of chairs,
a few tables with ratty-looking magazines, a row of
vending machines and a watercooler, all arranged
along what was essentially a wide hallway between
soundstages. He put on his shirt and took one of
the chairs.

An hour went by and then another. He struck
up conversations with some of the other applicants.
A crusty old guy named Wally Wilson told stories
about growing up on the Oklahoma prairie and riding the rodeos all over the West.

Potential contestants went through the door to
the soundstage, stayed awhile and came back out.
Some of them emerged from the interview and sat
down and waited, like Travis. Some left. Travis took

heart from the fact that he was among the ones asked to stay.

It was after six when they called him back in to tell him that he wouldn't be returning to Malibu that night—or any time soon, as it turned out. Real Deal Entertainment would put him up in a hotel room instead.

Travis lived in that hotel room for two weeks at Real Deal's beck and call. He took full advantage of room service, and he worked out in the hotel fitness center to pass the time while he got his background checked and his blood drawn. He even got interviewed by a shrink, who asked a lot of way-too-personal questions. There were also a series of follow-up meetings with casting people and producers. At the two-week mark, in a Century City office tower, he got a little quality time with a bunch of network suits.

That evening, absolutely certain he'd made the show, he raided the minibar in his room and raised a toast to his success.

Hot damn, he'd done it! He was going to be a contestant on *The Great Roundup*. He would have his shot at a cool million bucks.

And he would win, too. Damned if he wouldn't. He would build his own house on the family ranch and get more say in the day-to-day running of the place. His older brother, Anderson, made most of the decisions now. But if Travis had some hard cash to invest, his big brother would take him more seriously. Travis would step up as a real partner in running the ranch.

Being the good-time cowboy of the family had been fun. But there comes a point when every man has to figure out what to do with his life. Travis had reached that point. And *The Great Roundup* was going to take him where he needed to go.

The next morning, a car arrived to deliver him to the studio, where he sat in another waiting area outside a different soundstage with pretty much the same group of potential contestants he'd sat with two weeks before. One by one, they were called through the door. They all emerged smiling to be swiftly led away by their drivers.

When Travis's turn came, he walked onto the soundstage to find Giselle and Roxanne and a couple producers waiting at a long table. The camera was rolling. Except for that meeting in the office tower with the suits and a couple of sessions involving lawyers with papers to sign, a camera had been pointed at him every time they talked to him.

Giselle said, "Have a seat, Travis." He took the lone chair facing the others at the table. "We have some great news for you."

He knew it, he was in! He did a mental fist pump.

But then Giselle said, "You've made the cut for the final audition."

What the hell? *Another* audition?

"You'll love this, Travis." Giselle watched him expectantly as she announced, "The final audition will be in Rust Creek Falls."

Wait. What?

She went on, "As it happens, your hometown is not far from the supersecret location where *The Great Roundup* will be filmed. And since your first audition, we have been busy…"

Dirk Henley, one of the producers, chimed in. "We've been in touch with the mayor and the town council."

"Of Rust Creek Falls?" Travis asked, feeling dazed. He was still trying to deal with the fact that there was more auditioning to get through. He couldn't believe she'd just said the audition would be happening in his hometown.

"Of course of Rust Creek Falls." Giselle actually smiled, a smile that tried to be indulgent but was much too full of sharp white teeth to be anything but scary.

Dirk took over again. "Mayor Traub and the other council members are excited to welcome Real Deal Entertainment to their charming little Montana town."

Travis valiantly remained positive. Okay, he hadn't made the final cut, but he was still in the running and that was what mattered.

As for the final audition happening at home, well, now that he'd had a second or two to deal with that information, he supposed he wasn't all that surprised.

For a show like *The Great Roundup*, his hometown was a location scout's dream come true. And the mayor and the council would say yes to the idea in a New York minute. The movers and shakers of

Rust Creek Falls had gotten pretty ambitious in the last few years. They were always open to anything that might bring attention, money and/or jobs to town. Real Deal Entertainment should be good for at least the first two.

Dirk said, "We'll be sending Giselle, Roxanne, a camera crew *and* a few production people along with you for a last on-camera group audition."

Giselle showed more teeth. "We're going to put you and your fellow finalists in your own milieu, you might say."

Dirk nodded his approval. "And that milieu is a very atmospheric cowboy bar with which I'm sure you are familiar."

There was only one bar inside the Rust Creek Falls town limits. Travis named it. "The Ace."

"That's right!" Dirk beamed. "The Ace in the Hole, which we love."

What did that even mean? They loved the name? Must be it. No Hollywood type would actually *love* the Ace. It was a down-home, no-frills kind of place.

Dirk was still talking. "We'll be taking over 'the Ace'—" he actually air quoted it "—for a night of rollicking country fun. You know, burgers and brews and a country-western band. We want to see you get loose, kick over the traces, party in a purely cowboy sort of way. It will be fabulous. You're going to have a great time." He nodded at the other producer, who nodded right back. "I'm sure we'll get footage we can use on the show."

And then Giselle piped up with, "And, Travis…"

Her voice was much too casual, much too smooth. "We want you to bring your fiancée along to the audition. We love what you've told us about her, and we can't wait to meet her."

Chapter Two

*F*iancée?

Travis's heart bounced upward into his throat. He tried not to choke and put all he had into keeping his game face on.

But…

Fiancée? When did his imaginary girlfriend become a fiancée?

He'd never in his life had a fiancée. He hadn't even been with a woman in almost a year.

Yeah, all right. He had a rep as a ladies' man and he knew how to play that rep, but all that, with the women and the wild nights? It had gotten really old over time. And then there was what had happened last summer. After that, he'd realized he needed to grow the hell up. He'd sworn off women for a while.

Damn. This was bad. Much worse than finding out there was still another audition to get through. How had he not seen this coming?

Apparently, they'd decided they needed a little romance on the show, a young couple in love and engaged to be married—and he'd let Giselle get the idea that he could give them that. He'd thought he was playing the game, but he'd only played himself.

Giselle stood. "So, we're set then. You'll be taken back to the hotel for tonight. Pack up. Your plane leaves first thing tomorrow."

Ten of his fellow finalists were on that 7:00 a.m. flight to Salt Lake City the next day, including old Wally Wilson and the Franklins—Fred Franklin and his twin sons, Rob and Joey. Travis exchanged greetings with Wally, the Franklins and the rest of them, too.

He wasn't sitting near any of them, though. And the guy in the seat next to him dismissed Travis with a nod and spent the flight to Salt Lake City fiddling with his smartphone.

Travis stared out the window and considered his predicament.

A girl.

He needed a girl and he needed her fast.

Without one, he had a really bad feeling he wouldn't make the final *Great Roundup* cut.

At Salt Lake City International, they switched to a smaller plane that took them to Kalispell. Again, he got a seat next to a complete stranger. He stared out the window some more and gave himself a pep talk.

He'd come this far, and he wasn't about to give up now. Somehow, he needed to find himself a temporary fiancée. She had to be outgoing and pretty, someone who could rope and ride, build a campfire and handle a rifle, someone he could trust, someone he wouldn't mind pretending to be in love with.

And she had to be someone from town.

It was impossible. He knew that. But damn it, he was not giving up. Somehow, he had to find a way to give Giselle and the others what they wanted.

Real Deal Entertainment had a van waiting at the airport in Kalispell. The company had also sent along a production assistant, Gerry, to ride herd on the talent. Gerry made sure everyone and their luggage got on board the van and then drove them to Maverick Manor, a resort a few miles outside the Rust Creek Falls town limits.

Gerry herded them to the front desk. As he passed out the key cards, he announced that he was heading back to the airport to pick up the next group of finalists. They were to rest up and order room service. The producers and casting director would be calling everyone together first thing tomorrow right here in the main lobby.

Travis grabbed Gerry's arm before he could get away. "I need to go into town." *And rustle up a fiancée.*

Gerry frowned—but then he nodded. "Right.

You're Dalton, the local guy. You can get your own ride?"

"Yeah." A ride was the least of his problems.

Gerry regarded him, narrow eyed. Travis understood. As potential talent, the production company wanted him within reach at all times. He wouldn't be free again until he was either culled from the final cast list—or the show had finished shooting, whichever happened first.

Travis was determined not to be culled. "I'm supposed to bring my fiancée to the audition tomorrow night. I really need to talk to her about that." *As soon as I can find her.*

Gerry, who was about five foot six and weighed maybe 110 soaking wet, glared up at him. "Got it. Don't mess me up, man."

"No way. I *want* this job."

"Remember your confidentiality agreement. Nothing about the production or your possible part in it gets shared."

"I remember."

"Be in your room by seven tonight. I'll be checking."

"And I'll be there."

Gerry headed for the airport, and Travis called the ranch. His mother, Mary, answered the phone. "Honey, I am on my way," she said.

He was waiting at the front entrance of the manor when she pulled up in the battered pickup she'd been driving for as long as he could remember. She jumped out and grabbed him in a bear hug. "Two weeks in Hollywood hasn't done you any damage that I can see." She stepped back and clapped him on the arms. "Get in. Let's go."

She talked nonstop all the way back to the ranch—mostly about his father's brother, Phil, who had recently moved to town from Hardin, Montana. Phil Dalton had wanted a new start after the loss of Travis's aunt Diana. And Uncle Phil hadn't made the move alone. His and Diana's five grown sons had packed up and come with him.

At the ranch, Travis's mom insisted he come inside for a piece of her famous apple pie and some coffee.

"I don't have that long, Mom."

"Sit down," Mary commanded. "It's not gonna kill you to enjoy a slice of my pie."

So he had some pie and coffee. He saw his brother Anderson briefly. His dad, Ben, was still at work at his law office in town.

Zach, one of Uncle Phil's boys, came in, too. "That pie looks really good, Aunt Mary."

Mary laughed. "Sit down and I'll cut you a nice big piece."

Zach poured himself some coffee and took the chair across from Travis. In his late twenties, Zach was a good-looking guy. He asked Travis, "So how's it going with that reality show you're gonna be on?"

Travis kept it vague. "We'll see. I haven't made the final cut yet."

Zach shook his head. "Well, good luck. I don't get the appeal of all that glitzy Hollywood stuff. I'm more interested in settling down, you know? Since we lost Mom…" His voice trailed off, and his blue eyes were mournful.

"Oh, hon." Trav's mom patted Zach gently on the back. She returned to the stove and added over her shoulder, "It's a tough time, I know."

"So sorry about Aunt Diana," Travis said quietly.

Zach nodded. "Thank you both—and like I was sayin', losing Mom has reminded me of what really matters, made me see it's about time I found the right woman and started my family."

Travis ate another bite of his mother's excellent pie and then couldn't resist playing devil's advocate on the subject of settling down. "I can't even begin to understand how tough it's been for you and your dad and the other boys. But come on, Zach. You're not even thirty. What's the big hurry to go tying the knot?"

Zach sipped his coffee. "You would say that. From where I'm sitting, Travis, you're a little behind the curve. All your brothers and sisters—and more than a few cousins—are married and having babies. A wife and kids, that's what life's all about."

"I'll say it again. There's no rush." Well, okay. For him there kind of was. He needed a fiancée, yesterday or sooner. But a wife? Not any time soon.

Travis's mother spoke up from her spot at the stove. "Don't listen to him, Zach. If a wife is what you're looking for, you've come to the right place. There are plenty of pretty, smart, marriageable young women in Rust Creek Falls. Marriage is in the air around here."

Travis grunted. "Or it could be something in the water. Whatever it is, Mom's right. Marriage is nothing short of contagious in this town. Everybody seems to be coming down with it."

Zach forked up his last bite of pie. "Sounds like Rust Creek Falls is exactly the place that I want to be."

It was almost three in the afternoon when Travis climbed in his Ford F-150 crew cab and went to town. He had less than four hours before he had to be back in his room at Maverick Manor. Four hours to find his new fiancée.

He drove up and down the streets of town with the windows down, waving and calling greetings to people he knew, racking his brain for a likely candidate to play the love of his life on *The Great Roundup*.

Driving and waving were getting him nowhere. He decided he'd stop in at Daisy's Donut Shop, just step inside and see if his future fake fiancée might be waiting there, having herself a maple bar and coffee.

He found a spot at the curb in front of Buffalo Bill's Wings To Go, which was right next door to Daisy's. As he walked past, he stuck his head in Wings To Go. No prospects there. He went on to the donut shop, but when he peered in the window, he saw only five senior citizens and a young mother with two little ones under five.

Not a potential fiancée in sight.

Trying really hard not to get discouraged, he started to turn back for his truck. But then the door to the adjacent shop opened.

Callie Crawford, a nurse at the local clinic, came out of the beauty parlor. "Thanks, Brenna," Callie called over her shoulder before letting the door shut. She spotted Travis. "Hey, Travis! I heard about you and that reality show. Exciting stuff."

"Good to see you, Callie." He tipped his hat to her. "Final audition is tomorrow night."

"At the Ace, so I heard. We're all rooting for you."

He thanked her and asked her to say hi to her husband, Nate, for him. With a nod and a smile, Callie got in her SUV and drove off.

And that was it. That was when it happened. He watched Callie drive off down the street when it came to him.

Brenna. Brenna O'Reilly.

Good-looking, smart as a whip and raised on a ranch. She'd taken some ribbons barrel racing during the three or four summers she worked the local rodeo circuit. She was bold, too. Stood up for herself and didn't take any guff.

But he'd always considered himself too old for her. Plus, he kind of thought of himself as a guy who looked out for her. He would never make a move on her.

But this wouldn't be a move.

This would be…an opportunity.

If she was interested and if it was something she could actually handle.

Brenna.

Did he have any other prospects for this?

Hell, no.

He had less than three hours to find someone. At this point, it was pretty much Brenna or bust.

By then, he was already opening the door to the beauty shop. A bell tinkled overhead as he went in.

Brenna was standing right there, behind the reception counter with the cash register on it, facing the door. She looked kind of surprised at the sight of him.

Before either of them could say anything, the owner, Bee, spotted him. "Travis Dalton!" She waved at him with the giant blow-dryer in her left hand. "What do you know? It's our local celebrity."

Every woman in the shop turned to stare at him. He took off his hat and put on his best smile. "Not a celebrity *yet*, Bee. Ladies, how you doing?"

A chorus of greetings followed. He nodded and kept right on smiling.

Bee asked, "What can we do for you, darlin'?"

He thought fast. "The big final audition's tomorrow night."

"So we heard."

"Figured I could maybe use a haircut—just a trim." He hooked his hat on the rack by the door. "So, Brenna, you available?"

Brenna's blue eyes met his. "You're in luck.

I've got an hour before my next appointment." She came out from behind the counter, looking smart and sassy in snug jeans, ankle boots and a silky red shirt. Red worked for her. Matched her hair, which used to be a riot of springy curls way back when. Now she wore it straight and smooth, a waterfall of fire to just below her shoulders.

She waited until he'd hung up his denim jacket next to his hat then led him to her station. "Have a seat."

He dropped into the padded swivel chair and faced his own image in the mirror.

Brenna put her hands on his shoulders and leaned in. He got a whiff of her perfume. Nice. She caught his eye in the mirror and then ran her fingers up into his hair, her touch light, professional. "This looks pretty good."

It should. He'd paid a lot to a Hollywood stylist right before that first audition two weeks ago. "I was thinking just a trim."

She stood back, nodding, a dimple tucking into her velvety cheek as she smiled. "Well, all right. You want a shampoo first?"

What he wanted was to talk to her alone. He cast a glance to either side and lowered his voice. "Say, Brenna…"

She knew instantly that he was up to something. He could tell by the slight narrowing of her eyes and the way the bow of her upper lip flattened just a little. And then she leaned in again and whispered, "What's going on?"

He went for it. "I was wondering if I could talk to you in private."

Her sleek red-brown eyebrows drew together. "Right now?"

"Yeah."

"Where?"

He cast a quick glance around and spotted the hallway that led to the parking area in back. "Outside?"

She folded her arms across her chest and tipped her head to the side. "Sure. Go on out back. I'll be right there."

"Thanks." He got right up and headed for the back door, not even pausing to collect his jacket and hat. It wasn't that cold out, and he could get them later.

"What's going on?" Bee asked as he strode past her station.

Brenna answered for him. "Travis and I need to talk."

Somebody giggled.

Somebody else said, "Oh, I'll just bet you do."

Travis kept walking. It was okay with him if everyone at the beauty shop assumed he was finally making a move on Brenna—because he was.

Just not exactly in the way that they thought.

Outside, he looked for a secluded spot and settled on the three-walled nook where Bee stored her Dumpster. It didn't smell too bad, and the walls would give them privacy.

He heard the back door open again and stuck his head out to watch Brenna emerge. "Psst."

She spotted him and laughed. "Travis, what *is* this?"

He waved her forward. "Come on. We don't have all day."

For that he got an eye roll, but she did hustle on over to the enclosure. "All right, I'm here. Now what is it?"

He opened his mouth—and nothing came out. He had no idea where to even start.

"I…I have a proposal."

Her eyelashes swept down and then back up again. "Excuse me?"

"This… What I'm about to say. I need your solemn word you won't tell a soul about any of it, or I'll get sued for breach of contract. Understand?"

"Not really." She chewed on her lower lip for a moment. "But okay. I'm game. I won't tell a soul. You have my sworn word on that." She hooked her pinkie at him. He gave it a blank look. "Pinkie promise, Trav. You know that is the most solemn of promises and can never be broken."

"What are we, twelve?"

She made a little snorting sound. "Oh, come on."

He gave in and hooked his pinkie with hers. "Satisfied?"

"Are *you*? Because that is the question." She laughed, a sweet, musical sound, and tightened her pinkie against his briefly before letting go.

"As long as you promise me."

"Travis. I promise. I will tell no one, no matter what happens. Now what is going on?"

"How'd you like to be on *The Great Roundup*?"

She wrinkled her nose at him. "What? How? You're making no sense."

"Just listen, okay? Just give me a chance. I…well, I really thought I had it, you know? I thought I was on the show. But it turns out they want a young couple. A young, *engaged* couple. And the casting director sort of asked me if there was anyone special back home and I sort of said yes—and then, all of a sudden, they tell me there's one final audition, that it will be at the Ace and I should bring my fiancée."

Brenna's eyes were wide as dinner plates. "You told them you were *engaged*?"

"No, I didn't *tell* them that. They assumed it and I, well, I let them think it. And now I need a fake fiancée, okay? I need someone who doesn't mind putting herself out there, if you know what I mean. Someone who's not going to be afraid to speak up and hold her head high when the cameras are rolling. Someone good-looking who's familiar with ranch work, who can ride a horse and handle a rifle."

Brenna grinned then. "So you think I'm good-looking, huh?"

"Brenna, you're gorgeous."

"Travis." She looked like she was having a really good time. "Say that again."

Why not? It was only the truth. "Brenna, you are super fine."

And she threw back her red head and let her

laughter chime out. He stood there and watched her and thought how he'd known her since she was knee-high to a gnat. And that she was perfect, just what he needed to make Giselle happy—and earn him his spot on *The Great Roundup*.

But then she stopped laughing. She lowered her head and she regarded him steadily. "So say that it worked—say I go to the Ace with you tomorrow night and we convince them that we're together, that we're going to get married. Then what?"

"Then you belong to them for the next eight to ten weeks. First while they run checks on you and make sure you're healthy, mentally stable and have never murdered anyone or anything."

"You're not serious."

"As a rattler on a hot rock. And as soon as all that's over, we start filming. That's happening at some so far undisclosed Montana location. We're there until they're through filming."

"But what if I get eliminated? *Then* can I come home?"

He shook his head. "Everyone stays. So they can bring you back on camera if they want to, and also because if you come home early, everyone who knows you will know you've been eliminated. They want to keep the suspense going as to who the big winner is until the final show airs. Also, when the filming's over and you come home, you and I would still be pretending to be engaged."

"Until?"

"The episodes where we've each been eliminated

have aired—or the final episode, where one of us wins. The show airs once a week, August through December. Bottom line, you could be my fake fiancée straight through till Christmas."

She leaned against the wall next to the Dumpster and wrapped her arms around herself. "Wow. I... don't know what to say."

He resisted the burning need to promise her that they would win and that she was going to love it. "It's a lot to take in, I know."

She slanted him a glance. "I'd have to check with Bee, see if she'd hold my station for two months."

He knew Brenna was an independent contractor who rented a booth in the shop, but he refused to consider that Bee might say anything but yes. "I get that, sure."

"And then there's the money. I heard the winner gets a million dollars."

"Actually, once you get on the show, there's a graduated fee scale. The million is the top prize, but everybody gets something."

She leaned toward him a little, definitely interested. "Graduated how?"

"The first one eliminated gets twenty-five hundred. The longer you stay in the game, the more you get. For instance, if you last through the sixth show, you get ten thousand. And if you're the last to go before the winner, you get a hundred K."

She actually chuckled. "Good to know. So, Travis, if we're in this together, I say we split everything fifty-fifty."

He'd figured on giving her something, but he'd been kind of hoping she'd settle for much less. After all, he had big plans for his new house, for the ranch. He cleared his throat. "Would you take twenty percent?"

"Travis," she chided.

"Thirty?" he asked hopefully.

"Look at it this way. If they like me and want me on the show, you double your chances to win. Not to mention, the longer we both stay on, the more we both make." She spoke way too patiently. He found himself wistfully recalling the little girl she'd once been, the little girl who'd considered him her own personal hero and would have done anything he asked her to do, instantly, without question. Where had that little girl gone?

"True, but I'm your ticket in," he reminded her. "I'm the one who worked my ass off getting this far, you know?"

"I see that. And I admire that. I sincerely do. But without me, you won't make the cast."

She was probably right. He argued, anyway. "I'm not sure of that."

Brenna was silent, leaning there against the wall, her head tipped down. The seconds ticked by. He waited, trying to look easy and unconcerned, playing it like he didn't have a care in the world. Too bad that inside he was a nervous wreck.

Finally, she looked up and spoke again. "I'm trying not to be so impulsive in my life, to settle down a little, you know what I mean?"

Their eyes met and they gazed at each other for a long count of ten. "Bren. I know exactly what you mean."

She gave a chuckle, sweet and low. "I kind of thought that you might. The thing is, playing your fake fiancée on a reality show is not exactly what I would call settling down. And what are the odds against us, anyway? How many will end up competing with us?"

"I think there are twenty-two contestants total, so it's you and me and twenty others."

"Meaning that however we split the money, odds are someone else will take home the big prize."

He pushed off the wall, took her by the shoulders and looked deeply into those ocean-blue eyes. "First rule. Never, *ever* say we might not win. We *will* win. Half the battle is the mental game. Defeat is not an option. Winning is the only acceptable outcome."

She got it, she really did. He could feel it in the sudden straightening of her shoulders beneath his hands, see it in the bright gleam that lit those wide eyes. "Yeah. You're right. We *will* win."

"That's it. Hold that thought." He let go of her shoulders but held her gaze.

She said, "We really would be increasing our chances, the two of us together. Together, we can work out strategies, you know? We can plan how to handle whatever they throw at us."

"Exactly. We would have each other's backs. So what do you say, Bren?"

"I still want half the money." A gust of wind

slipped into the three-sided enclosure and stirred her hair, blowing a few fiery strands across her mouth.

He smoothed them out of the way, guiding them behind her ear, thinking how soft her pale skin was and marveling at how she'd grown up to be downright hot. It was a good thing he'd always promised himself he'd never make a move on her. Add that promise to the fact that he'd sworn off women and he should be able to keep from getting any romantic ideas about her.

"Travis?" She searched his face. "Did you hear what I just said?"

"I heard." He ordered his mind off her inconvenient hotness and set it on coming up with more reasons she should take less than half the prize.

Unfortunately, he couldn't think of a single one.

So all right, then. His new house and his investment in the ranch would be smaller. But his chances of winning had just doubled—*more* than doubled. Because Brenna was a fighter, and together they *would* go all the way to the win.

"Fair enough, Bren. Fifty-fifty, you and me." He held up his hand.

She slapped a high five on it. "I'll be right back."

He caught her before she could get away. "There's more we need to talk about."

"Not until I get the okay from Bee, we don't." She glanced down at his fingers wrapped around her upper arm.

He let go. "What will you say to her?"

"That I might have a chance on *The Great Roundup*,

but to try for it, I need to know that she'll let me have my booth back on August 1."

"Good. That's good. Don't mention the engagement yet. We still need to decide how to handle that."

She let out another sweet, happy laugh—and then mimed locking her mouth and tossing away the key. "My lips are sealed," she whispered, then whirled on her heel and headed for the back door.

Five endless minutes later, she returned.

"Well?" he asked, his heart pounding a worried rhythm beneath his ribs.

Her smile burst wide open. "Bee wished us luck."

"And?"

"Yes, she'll hold my booth for me."

He almost grabbed her and hugged her, but caught himself in time. "Excellent."

"Yeah—and is there some reason we need to hang around out here? Let's go in. I'll give you that trim you pretended you needed."

He heard a scratching sound, boots crunching gravel. "What's that?"

"What?"

He signaled for silence and stuck his head out of the enclosure in time to see the back of crazy old Homer Gilmore as he scuttled away across the parking lot toward the community center on Main, the next street over.

Brenna stuck her head out, too. "It's just Homer."

They retreated together back into the enclosure. He asked, "You think he heard us?"

She was completely unconcerned. "Even if he did, Homer's not going to say anything."

"And you know this how?"

"He's a little odd, but he minds his own business."

"A *little* odd? He's the one who spiked the punch with moonshine at Braden and Jennifer's wedding two years ago."

"So?" The wind stirred her hair again. She combed it back off her forehead with her fingers. "He never gossips or carries tales. To tell you the truth, I trust him."

"Because...?"

"It's just, well, I don't know. I have this feeling that he looks out for me, like a guardian angel or a fairy godmother."

Travis couldn't help scoffing, "One who just happens to be a peculiar old homeless man."

"Trav," she insisted, "he's not going to say anything. I guarantee it. Now, let's go in and—"

He put up a hand. "Just a minute. A couple more things. Starting tomorrow night, we're madly in love. You'll need to convince a bunch of LA TV people that I'm the only guy for you."

"Well, that's a lot to ask," she teased. "But I'll do my best."

"You'll need to make everyone in town believe it, too—including your family. They all have to think we're for real."

"Trav, I can do it." She was all determination now. "You can count on me."

"That's what I needed to hear."

"Then can we go in?"

"There's one more thing…"

"What?"

"It's important tomorrow night that you be on. You need to show them your most outgoing self. Sell your own personality." When she nodded up at him, he went on, "I did a lot of research on reality shows before I went into this. What I learned is that the show is a story, Bren. A story told in weekly episodes. And a good story is all about big personalities, characters you can't forget, over-the-top emotions. What I'm saying is, you can't be shy. It's better to embarrass yourself than to be all bottled up and boring. Are you hearing what I'm saying?"

"Yes, I am. And let me ask you something. When have you ever known me to be boring?"

Her various escapades over the years scrolled through his mind. At the age of nine, she'd gotten mad at her mom and run away. She got all the way to Portland, Oregon, before they caught up with her. At twelve, she'd coldcocked one of the Peabody boys when she caught him picking on a younger kid. Peabody hit the ground hard. It took thirty stitches to sew him back up. At sixteen, she'd rolled her pickup over a cliff because she never could resist a challenge and Leonie Parker had dared her to race up Fall Mountain. Only the good Lord knew how she'd survived that crash without major injury.

The more Travis thought of all the crazy things she'd done, the more certain he became that Brenna

O'Reilly would have no problem selling herself to Giselle and the rest of them. "All right. I hear you."

"Good. 'Cause I'm a lot of things, Travis Dalton. But I am *never* shy or boring."

The next night, Real Deal Entertainment had assigned Gerry to drive the finalists to the Ace in the Hole.

All except for Travis. They let him make a quick trip to Kalispell in the afternoon and then, in the evening, he drove his F-150 out to the O'Reilly place to pick up his supposed fiancée.

Brenna's mom answered his knock. Travis had always liked Maureen O'Reilly. She loved her life on the family ranch, and her kitchen was the heart of her home. She'd always treated Travis with warmth and affection.

Tonight, however? Not so much. When he swept off his hat and gave her a big smile, she didn't smile back.

"Hello, Travis." Maureen pulled back the door and then hustled him into the living room, where she offered him a seat on the sofa. "Brenna will be right down."

"Great. Thanks."

She leaned toward him a little and asked in a low voice, "Travis, I need you to be honest with me. What's going on here?"

Before he left Brenna at the beauty shop yesterday, they'd agreed on how to handle things with her parents and his. Right now, Maureen needed to know that there was *something* going on between him and her middle daughter. The news of their engagement, however, would come a little bit later. "Brenna and I have a whole lot in common. She's agreed to come out to the audition at the Ace with me tonight."

"What does that mean, 'a whole lot in common'?"

"I care for her. I care for her deeply." It was surprisingly easy to say. Probably because it was true. He did care for Brenna. Always had. "She's one of a kind. There's no other girl like her."

Maureen scowled. She opened her mouth to speak again, but before she got a word out, her husband, Paddy, appeared in the archway that led to the kitchen.

"Travis. How you doin'?"

"Great, Paddy." He popped to his feet, and he and Paddy shook hands. "Real good to see you."

"Heard about you and that reality show."

"Final audition is tonight."

"Well, good luck to you, son."

Maureen started to speak again, but Brenna's arrival cut her off. "It's show business, Dad," she scolded with a playful smile. "In show business, you say 'break a leg.'"

Travis tried not to stare as she came down the steps wearing dark-wash jeans that hugged her strong legs and a sleeveless lace-trimmed purple top that clung to every curve. Damn, she was fine. Purple suede dress boots and a rhinestone-studded cowboy hat completed the perfect picture she made.

Again, Travis reminded himself that she was spunky little Brenna O'Reilly and this so-called relationship they were going to have when they got on the show was just that—all show. Brenna didn't need to be messing with a troublesome cowboy like him.

And he knew very well that Maureen thought so, too.

Still, he could almost start having *real* ideas about Brenna and him and what they might get up to together pretending to be engaged during *The Great Roundup*.

Brenna kissed her mom on the cheek and then her dad, too. She handed Travis her rhinestone-trimmed jean jacket and he helped her into it.

They managed to get out the door and into the pickup without Maureen asking any more uncomfortable questions.

"It's time," she said in a low and angry tone as he turned off the dirt road from the ranch and onto the highway heading toward town. "Scratch that. It's *past* time I got my own place." Rentals in Rust Creek Falls were hard to come by. A lot of young women like Brenna lived with their parents until they got married or scraped together enough to buy something of their own. "Bee offered me her apartment over the beauty shop. She's been living in Kalispell, anyway, with her new guy. So when we win *The Great Roundup*, I'm moving. I love my mom, but she's driving me crazy."

"*When we win.* That's the spirit." As for Maureen, he played the diplomat. "Your mom's a wonderful woman."

Brenna shook her head and stared out the window. He almost asked her exactly what Maureen might have said to upset her—but then again, it was probably about him and he wasn't sure he wanted to know.

The rest of the ride passed in silence. Travis wanted to give Brenna a little more coaching on how to become a reality TV star, but the closer they got to town, the more withdrawn she seemed. He started to worry that something was really bothering her—something more than annoyance with her mom. And he had no idea what to say to ease whatever weighed on her mind.

The parking lot at the Ace was full. Music poured out of the ramshackle wooden building at the front of the lot. They were playing a fast one, something with a driving beat. Travis drove up and down the rows of parked vehicles, looking for a free space. Finally, in the last row at the very back of the lot, he found one.

He pulled in and turned off the engine. "You okay, Brenna?"

She aimed a blinding smile at him. "Great. Let's get going." She opened her door and swung those purple boots to the dirt and got out.

So he jumped out on his side and hustled around to her. He offered his hand. She gave him the strangest wild-eyed sort of look, but then she took it. Hers was ice-cold. He laced their fingers together and considered pulling her back, demanding to know if she was all right.

"Let's do this." She started walking, head high,

that red hair shining down her back, rhinestones glittering on her hat, along the cuffs, hem and collar of her pretty denim jacket.

He fell in step with her, though he had a scary premonition they were headed straight for disaster. She seemed completely determined to go forward. He was afraid to slow her down, afraid that would finish her somehow, that calling a halt until she told him what was wrong would only make her turn and run. Their chance on *The Great Roundup* would be lost before they even got inside to try for it.

They went around to the front of the building and up the wooden steps. A couple of cowboys came out and held the door for them. Both men looked at Brenna with interest, and Travis felt a buzz of irritation under his skin. He gave them each a warning glare. The men tipped their hats and kept on walking.

Inside, it was loud and wall-to-wall with partiers. Travis had never seen the Ace this packed. He spotted a couple of cameramen filming the crowd. Over by the bar, he caught sight of Wally Wilson talking the ear off one of the bartenders. And another finalist, that platinum-blonde rodeo star, Summer Knight, was surrounded by cowboys. He knew it was her by the shine of her almost-white hair and that sexy laugh of hers.

"Come on." He pulled Brenna in closer so she could hear him. "We'll find the casting director, Giselle. I'll introduce you."

She blinked and stared at him through those now-enormous eyes. What was going on with her? She really didn't look good.

Brenna was nervous.

Well, okay. Beyond nervous. Actually, she was freaking out. Brenna never freaked out.

And that freaked her out even more.

She'd been so sure she knew how to handle herself. She *did* know how to handle herself. She was bold. Fearless. Nothing scared her. Ever.

Except this, the Ace packed to bursting, the music so loud. All these people pressing in around her, a casting director waiting to meet her.

And Travis.

Travis, who was counting on her to win them both a spot on *The Great Roundup*.

Dear Lord, she didn't want to blow this. She would never forgive herself if she let Travis down.

"There's Giselle." Travis waved at a tall, model-skinny woman on the other side of the room. The woman lifted a hand and signaled them to join her. "This way." His fingers still laced with hers, he started working his way through the crowd, leading her toward the tall woman with cheekbones so sharp they threatened to poke right through her skin.

"Wait." Brenna dug in her boot heels.

He stopped and turned back to her, a worried frown between his eyebrows. "Bren?" He said her name softly, gently. He knew she was losing it. "What? Tell me."

She blasted a smile at him and forced a brittle laugh. "Can you just give me a minute?" She tipped her head toward the hallway that led to the ladies' room. "I'll be right back." She tugged free of his grip.

"Brenna—"

"I need to check my lip gloss."

"But—"

"Right back." She sent him a quick wave over her shoulder and made for the hallway, scattering *Excuse me*s as she went, weaving her way as fast as she could through the tight knots of people, ignoring anyone who spoke to her or glanced her way.

When she reached the hallway, she kept on going, her eyes on the glowing green exit sign down at the end. She got to the ladies' room and she didn't even slow down. She just kept right on walking down to the end of the hall.

And out the back door.

Don't miss
THE MAVERICK FAKES A BRIDE
by Christine Rimmer,
available July 2017 wherever
Harlequin® Special Edition books
and ebooks are sold.

www.Harlequin.com

#2557 THE MAVERICK FAKES A BRIDE!
Montana Mavericks: The Great Family Roundup
by Christine Rimmer
Travis Dalton needs a fake fiancée fast, or he'll be cut from the final cast of a cowboy reality show. Bold, adventurous Brenna O'Reilly is perfect for the role. Too bad pretending they're lovers for the cameras quickly has Travis and Brenna wishing this game of love would never have to end.

#2558 A SECOND CHANCE FOR THE SINGLE DAD
Matchmaking Mamas • by Marie Ferrarella
Dr. Luke Dolan is a recently widowed, floundering single dad who also happens to need a nurse for his new practice. Lucky for him, the Matchmaking Mamas know just who to call! Kayley Quartermain is a nurse looking for direction and perhaps a happy ending of her very own...

#2559 SAY YES TO THE COWBOY
Thunder Mountain Brotherhood • by Vicki Lewis Thompson
Tess Irwin is elated to find herself pregnant, though not so much about the fact that Zeke Rafferty is the father. But the former foster child can't turn his back on his child. Can they work out a visitation compromise without getting their hearts broken in the process?

#2560 A BRIDE, A BARN, AND A BABY
Celebration, TX • by Nancy Robards Thompson
Lucy Campbell is thrilled Zane Phillips finally sees her as more than his friend's little sister. Until she gets pregnant! Refusing to trap him into marriage, she rejects his proposal. But Zane is beginning to realize he just might want everything Lucy has to offer after all.

#2561 IT STARTED WITH A DIAMOND
Drake Diamonds • by Teri Wilson
When Diana Drake, a diamond heiress, and Franco Andrade, a disgraced polo player, pretend to be engaged for their own selfish reasons, their charade soon becomes more real than either of them intended.

#2562 HOME TO WICKHAM FALLS
Wickham Falls Weddings • by Rochelle Alers
Sawyer Middleton swore he would never return to his hometown, but when a family emergency forces his hand, he meets Jessica Calhoun, an intriguing teacher who has *forever* written all over her. Will this free-wheeling city boy give up his fast-paced life in the face of love?

HSECNM0617

SPECIAL EXCERPT FROM

HQN™

A rising-star art investigator finds herself captivated by Icon, an enigmatic international art thief whose heists are methodical, daring, baffling. To Zara the case is maddening—bordering on an obsession. She finds distraction in the arms of a magnetic American billionaire but, as she surrenders to his captivating allure and glamorous world, she must determine if it's the real thing…or just a convincing forgery.

Enjoy a sneak peek of
*THE CHASE, the first book in the **ICON** series*
by USA TODAY bestselling author Vanessa Fewings.

My gaze fixed on the living, breathing sculpture.

My heartbeat quickened as I searched my memory for where I knew him from. I was awestruck by this breathtaking Adonis, who was reaching for a white shirt hanging on the back of a chair. He was tall and devastatingly handsome in a rugged kind of way. Thirty, maybe? Those short, dark golden locks framing a gorgeous face, his three-day stubble marking him with a tenacious edge and that thin wry smile exuding a fierce confidence. His intense, steady glare stayed on mine as he calmly pulled his arm through a sleeve and covered that tattoo before I could make out more.

A gasp caught in my throat as it came to me that we'd never actually met, probably because this was Tobias William Wilder, a billionaire. He moved in the kind of refined circles one would expect from a business magnate and inventor who owned TechRule, one of the largest software companies in the world.

And I'd given this playboy mogul his very own peep show.

I'd read an article on him, featuring his Los Angeles–based art gallery, The Wilder. It was an acclaimed museum that was one of the most prestigious in the world.

Although I'd imagined one day I might bump into him with the art world being relatively small, never had I imagined a scenario as racy as this.

"I'm looking for the stairs," I managed.

"That way." His refined American accent felt like another blow to my reason.

That alpha-maleness made him look like he'd just returned from a dangerous adventure in the Himalayas or even the jungles of Peru…

A waft of expensive musky cologne reached me with its sensuous allure and did something crazy to my body.

"You might want to put some clothes on," I said firmly.

"Well, now I'm dressed."

Yes, he was, and this was a changing room, apparently, and I'd not exactly represented a pillar of virtue.

"Well that's good." I swallowed my pride. "Please keep it that way."

His gaze lowered to my feet.

And I remembered my strappy stilettos were flirtatiously dangling from my left hand, those spiked heels hinting at a sexy side I wished I had.

Intrigue marred his face, and then his expression softened again as his jade gaze returned to hold mine.

I left in a rush, shaken with just how this man had affected me merely with a smile.

I felt an inexplicable need to run back in and continue to bathe in the aura of the most enigmatic man I'd ever met.

Will Zara risk it all when she finds herself on a collision course with danger and desire?

Find out when THE CHASE by USA TODAY bestselling author Vanessa Fewings goes on sale in June 2017.

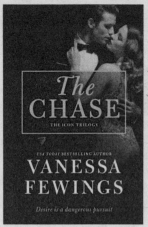

THE WORLD IS BETTER WITH

WITH

Romance

Harlequin has everything from contemporary, passionate and heartwarming to suspenseful and inspirational stories.

Whatever your mood,
we have a romance just for you!

Connect with us to find your next great read, special offers and more.

 /HarlequinBooks

@HarlequinBooks

www.HarlequinBlog.com

www.Harlequin.com/Newsletters

HARLEQUIN®

A *Romance* FOR EVERY MOOD™

www.Harlequin.com

Turn your love of reading into rewards you'll love with
Harlequin My Rewards